Wakefield Press

the Goddamn Bus of Happiness

Stefan Laszczuk was born in 1973. He lives in Adelaide.
In 2002 he published *The New Cage*, a book of short stories.
The Goddamn Bus of Happiness is his first novel. He plays
in local bands *krystapinzch* and *simpleman*.

the Goddamn Bus of Happiness

Stefan Laszczuk

Wakefield Press

Wakefield Press
1 The Parade West
Kent Town
South Australia 5067
www.wakefieldpress.com.au

First published 2005
Copyright © Stefan Laszczuk, 2005

Cover designed by Liz Nicholson, DesignBITE
Text designed and typeset by Ryan Paine, Wakefield Press
Printed and bound by Hyde Park Press

National Library of Australia
Cataloguing-in-publication entry

Laszczuk, Stefan, 1973– .
The goddamn bus of happiness.

ISBN 1 86254 649 5.

I. Title.

A823.4

Publication of this book was assisted by the
Commonwealth Government through the
Australia Council, its arts funding and advisory body.

Margaritai Biezaitei

Mūsu dārzā—staltākais koks,
krāšņākais zieds

contents

Chapter one
The mark of a man

A freak deep breath swells my lungs like post-accident airbags. The dull ache in my chest sharpens to an invisible stab. I wince and swallow foul residue. Stare through an all-too-familiar haze at my parents' front yard. Their garden gnome is still smiling, though he's now missing an arm.

Across the street Mrs Beveringham the local Neighbourhood Watch freak is peering through her window. Nina doesn't like being spied on. She keeps looking straight ahead but she raises a middle finger in Mrs Beveringham's general direction.

'Neen!' I pull her arm down. She screws up her face and pokes out her tongue at no one in particular. I look apologetically at Mrs Beveringham. Her face is set in unimpressed stone. It's Mrs Beveringham's favourite expression. And it watches us all the way to my parents' front door.

We're late. We've just come from visiting Neen's dad—meaning Neen's been at his grave for about an hour and I've been waiting for her in the car. I always wait in the car when we visit him. Neen doesn't like anyone to see her cry. I don't mind hanging out on my own in the car. I don't even mind the heat or the fact the car radio doesn't work. I don't mind sitting and staring out the window for an hour—as long as I'm doing it for her.

Today the cemetery was full of people. I was pretty full myself and there was nowhere to sneak a piss so I had to fill up an empty coke bottle I found under the seat. I was lucky it was there. Nina'd already cleared out a few. Stuffed them with dodgy flowers to put in front of her dad's headstone. She left one dodgy flower behind for me. Always does. And I always take it home and stick it to our lounge room wall: our magnificent dried-out dodgy-flower hanging garden.

The coke bottle's sticking out of my jacket pocket now. Neen didn't want me to leave it in her car in case I forgot to take it with me later. There's something about carrying around a bottle full of my own urine that's unnerving me. Perhaps it's because I'm about to sit down and have a serious talk with my parents. A serious talk about my younger sister. They think she's been getting up to no good. As far as I know, my sister is doing nothing more than building a solid reputation as a babysitter. At some time or other she's responsible for just about every kid in the neighbourhood. I saw her ad in the community rag the other day:

Jane the babysitter.
Cheap rates.

Good with kids.
Used to be one.

Short, sharp and to the point. Just like Janey. She gets her jobs mainly through ads like that, and through meeting the parents of the young tennis hopefuls she coaches after school. Staying at school and holding down two jobs is good stuff for a sixteen-year-old. I'm proud of her. Still, although our parents appear tentatively proud too, they don't cut her much slack. They're always on at her to try harder, reach further, fear less. Dad in particular has been hell bent on instilling his 'good chocca rules for success' in Janey since resigning himself to accepting my own antithetic approach.

Dad and his idea of success. He won a fake silver medallion in 1974 for building the second-best campfire in the Panorama Sea Scout 'Oar-lympics' and he's barely stopped talking about it since. He's damn proud of that painted silver medallion. Damn proud even though I point out he was in the Sea Scouts and that his skills should have been making sails or building boats or something sea-ish. Even though I point out there were only two goddamn competitors in the campfire-building event anyway. He remains damn proud even when his mates drop around to drink a quick beer and have a quick smirk and make a few jibes about the fact that he's still got his medallion hanging in pride of place above the mantelpiece in his living room.

'It's all about the principle,' he says to them, and to me, as he knocks back his can of beer. 'It's all about having a crack at something.'

He probably thinks that his attitude is inspiring but it has totally the opposite effect on me. The last thing I'd ever want is a disintegrating medallion with my name spelt wrong stuck over my mantelpiece for the rest of my life. Then again, who am I to talk? My own recent achievements amount to nothing but a plastic container full of piss in my pocket. God, I hope my mum doesn't see it sticking out like that. I reach in and put my hand around it and put my free arm around the woman next to me.

'You okay Neen?'

'Yeah, yeah, of course. I'm fine.' She rolls her eyes. I was worried about bringing her here straight after visiting her dad. I shouldn't have been. She's good at letting herself grieve and then getting on with life. It's a skill I'm still learning.

Mum unlocks the screen door looking serious and says she's really glad we could both make it, even though we're late. She says we need to have a talk about Jane and that we should be all right for a while because Jane's out babysitting.

'Who needs babies sat on a Sunday afternoon?'

Mum says that poor Mr Jessop does.

Harvey Jessop lives four doors down. He's a fifty-three-year-old balding, badly dressed dentist who moved here from America when his wife died six years ago. He's been 'poor' Mr Jessop since he told Mum and Dad about how the good Lord took his wife, Henrietta, who he claims to have loved 'more'n a Sat'dee afternoon chilli hotdog'.

Quite frankly I find it hard to sympathise with a man who compares his life partner to processed offal wrapped in a sugary bun. But credit where it's due. He's determined to work through his grief and raise their son, their bucket of hot chips. The child they had together before Henrietta was decapitated by a wayward garbage truck. It'll be tough but he'll raise the kid good, he tells my parents.

After he finds out about poor Mr Jessop's wife, my dad takes me aside one afternoon, knocks back the rest of a beer, looks me in the eye and tells me that Mr Jessop's courage to get on with the business of raising a child after such a tragedy is the mark of the man—a man who chooses to keep running the marathon of life, even though he has to run the last half alone. Mum agrees. In fact she agrees so wholeheartedly that when she gets a phone call from poor Mr Jessop asking for her daughter's babysitting services, she even offers to pay the first month of Janey's wages for him as a show of support. Not to be outdone, Dad chimes in and offers to mow Jessop's lawns once a month—'got to run a few miles with the man, son.' And Janey starts going around there every Sunday from then on.

So Janey's babysitting for Mr Jessop every Sunday afternoon and giving tennis lessons every Tuesday. And she has other babysitting gigs. She's working hard. Mum sits there and tells me and tells Nina that would explain why Janey has more money than she used to. But Mum's not stupid, she tells us. She says she's smart enough not to need an explanation as to why she found more than two thousand dollars in a shoebox under Janey's bed the other day. She knows that kind of money under a sixteen-year-old's bed spells one thing. In case we don't understand she leans back in her chair and spells it for us: 'D-R-U-G-S.'

She says she doesn't need us to tell her that Janey's involved in drugs. She just needs us to help get Janey uninvolved. She says that with my history as an anti-authoritarian and Nina's history as a teenage girl, the two of us should be able to put our heads together and come up with something.

Nina, true to form, wants to help. Myself, I'm not exactly sure how I can—but Mum persists. 'You must know about these things, Mico,' she says. 'You can help us with this.' My dad nods. 'We need you on this, son.'

And so I manage to ignore the fact that I've barely touched illegal substances at all in my life. I ignore the disturbing assumption my parents have made that I must be some sort of expert on drugs because I used to have long hair and once went to a peace rally. I accept their invitation to be a Sunday afternoon drug expert, even if it means I am going to have to lie a bit. Even if it means delaying my planned session in the beer garden with my mate Couper who, when I think about it, is actually the perfect person to come around and give advice on how to kick drug habits. Well, sort of kick 'em.

So we sit at the dining room table and I tell what I know about drugs and drug-selling, which is not a lot. But even though Nina has to correct me more than a few times, I still manage to come off sounding like some sort of authority.

Nina tries to give my parents the bigger picture. She tells them the problem isn't just drugs. That it's also got to do with Janey being a teenager. She tells them what it's like to be a teenage girl and about all the peer pressure that goes with it. She tells them about the recklessness and the early experimentation and the early sex and the things that teenage girls think they can get away with. Even I'm a smidgen uncomfortable with her level of frankness, despite my knowledge of her particularly wild childhood. And, to be honest, I start hoping she'll get away from the bigger picture and get back to drugs. I think my parents are hoping so as well. Dad starts shifting awkwardly in his seat. I can see he's beginning to wonder whether this is such a good idea.

Just as I think Mum's about to have a seizure, Nina gives a reassuring smile and says not to worry, she's just trying to explain some of the difficult choices that teenage girls face and that it's possible to remain sensible despite peer group pressure. After all, she lies, she herself managed to avoid succumbing to temptation. When she says that, I can literally see the relief wash over my parents' faces and I even feel a tiny wave of approval that I haven't felt since I lied myself and told them I vote Liberal. Of course, Nina doesn't mention she used to be a dope addict and that she's been having regular sex since she was fourteen. My parents wouldn't even understand that kind of behaviour, let alone condone it. No siree. Ragmilla and Stan didn't have intercourse until they were well and truly married—and they've never even *thought* about touching illegal substances. If you think that sounds a little conservative, keep this in mind: my mum thinks a 'bong' is the sound a bell makes and my dad thinks a 'dildo' is a bird that went extinct in the late seventeenth century.

So Mum and Dad try and act as if they already know most of the stuff we're telling them but interject every now and then with a question that would try the patience of a twelve-year-old. When we're finished, my mum asks, 'So what do you think we should do?'

I suggest they calmly ask Janey her feelings about drugs and then listen to what she says without judgement or hostility—the same way they're listening to me right now.

Nina agrees. 'Give her a chance to make her own decision,' she says. 'She's probably not in as deep as you think. And she's a smart kid, she'll make the right choice in the end.' Nina's good like that. She's got the greatest respect for young people. She thinks pretty much everyone will turn out okay if they're given a chance.

Mum says that while it might be okay to talk about

drugs with *me*, the thing about Janey is that she's got such a bright future. Before I can ask her what the thing about *me* is, Dad says he's had enough insight into the minds of teenage girls for one day and he's going to the local and I can come if I've got nothing better to do. There's a silence. We all know that this is the first time he's asked me to join him, as an equal, in his sacred local front bar. When I was young he used to take me to front bars all the time and I would sit and play Space Invaders while he sank beers with the boys and bet on the races. But he hasn't asked me out for a drink, just me and him, since I reached legal age. Maybe it's because of the way he saw me carry on at my eighteenth birthday party when I had too much to drink. When half the party laughed and whistled and cheered and the other half looked awkwardly at the floor as I dragged my thirty-year-old equally shit-faced hairdresser behind the dry ice machine and tried to stick my hand down the front of her fishnets. Perhaps Dad decided then and there that I would have to prove myself to be a more responsible man before he allowed me to join him in his front bar. Perhaps he wanted me to learn a certain manly code of behaviour before he would trust me enough to claim me as his son in front of the tough old dogs that are his front bar pals.

I don't know why he suddenly makes the decision that I've become responsible enough to join him now, almost immediately after I tell him I know where to get some blow. But however surprised I am that it's my supposed knowledge of drugs, not my abhorrence of them, that raises my stature in my father's eyes, I'm not about to complain. It's been a long time between drinks for a guy and his old man. I'll take what I can get. And anyway, I feel like a beer.

So we get to the pub and Dad buys me a schooner and I comment on the good head and he gives me a half-smile. Then Bob the butcher comes over. He's holding a fresh pint of Caffrey's and wearing a frothy grin. Bob doesn't see me and Dad doesn't point me out. He just turns slightly away and they start talking horses. The half-smile has been replaced by a familiar, thick, almost belligerent, side-on stance that instantly makes me feel as if I'm intruding. I should have seen it coming. I turn away to find myself once again looking at a computer game. It's not Space Invaders though. These days the only thing around here that looks like a Space Invader is me. I'm an invader of my dad's space and for some reason he won't tell me how not to be one. So I stand there in his front bar and stare at a computer game and listen to him discuss the track form with Bob.

It makes for mind-numbing eavesdropping but there's not much else I can do here on my own—and let's face it, I'm on my own. I won't lay a bet because I never win. I can't even just chug the beers down because I hardly brought any money with me and I don't want to have to ask Dad for more. Anyway, I don't really feel like hanging out here all afternoon. Dad's front bar is a dive. Perhaps that's the real reason he's never invited me here before—he's ashamed of this dingy little room where he spends so much of his time. I'll never know though and I don't really even care. To be honest, I think I'd rather be shit-faced behind a dry ice machine. Tangled and slapped. Noticed.

So I'm watching Dad enjoying his beer with Bob the butcher, looking up at the TAB screen, when Race 4 at Randwick starts. The old man's staring up at the screen yelling 'GO PUMPERNICKEL! GO YOU GOOD THING!' when something Bob must have said a few minutes back appears to have stood out from the clutter of the afternoon's conversations and finally registered in Dad's brain. Suddenly he stops yelling 'GO PUMPERNICKEL!' and starts yelling 'NEVER MARRIED? NEVER HAD CHILDREN? NEVER MARRIED?' and he's not yelling at the screen anymore. He's yelling at Bob the butcher. 'NEVER HAD CHILDREN?' Other blokes are looking around with rare front bar agitation and it's probably only my dad's proud and long history of observing front bar etiquette that stops any of them telling him to shut the fuck up or get the fuck out. Bob's kind of shrugging and nodding and then Dad downs the last of his schooner and slams the glass on the bar and barks at me across the room 'NOW MICO!' which he hasn't done since he used to stop me playing in the middle of my Space Invaders game.

And as I follow him towards the door he turns and looks past me and yells over my shoulder 'YOU BLOODY

SURE? NEVER HAD CHILDREN?' and Bob the butcher nods in bewilderment as if my dad had asked him if ham comes from pigs and suddenly Pumpernickel's running a distant third to Dad and me hitting the fresh air outside.

In five minutes we're at Mr Jessop's. Dad doesn't bother going to the front door. Instead he stomps across the thickish front lawn towards the side gate. I'm tempted to point out it could do with a mow, but I keep my mouth shut and follow my dad, even though I don't understand where we're going. Even though right now, more than ever, he doesn't know I exist. As we go through the side gate I can hear the thump, thump, thump of a tennis ball against a wall. Then the thumping against the wall stops and the thumping in my heart starts as I round the corner to see my sixteen-year-old sister like I never have before. And now I understand where we're going.

Janey's wearing a black G-string bikini and swinging a tennis racket with that iron grip of hers. She sees us and stops, stands there open-mouthed, stunned. A tennis ball rolls silently past her slender, tanned feet. I look up to see that less than four metres away, Mr Jessop has just dribbled on his kitchen window. It's the mark of the man. He's not so much running in the marathon of life as he is kneeling on the kitchen bench of marble, with his pants around his ankles, a glass of Campari and soda in one hand and his fifty-three-year-old drooping sticky cock in the other. He doesn't see me and Dad standing at the side of his back courtyard. Doesn't see Dad's initial confusion become anger. He only has eyes for Janey.

Even though he only has eyes for Janey, I'm pretty sure he sees my father briefly before he's lying on his back on the slate kitchen floor among broken glass and spilt Campari soda. And I bet nearly the whole neighbourhood has *ears* for Janey, as she's carried away by my father's own iron grip around her wrist, screaming that she was only practising tennis. 'Hitting balls against a fucking wall!'

Dad roars back 'Bullfuckingshit!' and that next thing she'll have someone hitting balls against her chin. Then he calls her a whore and she screams 'Fuck you!' and he hits her for the first time in over a decade. I follow them as he drags her back out the side gate. He doesn't bother trying to put her in the car, just hoists her over his shoulder. I bet half the people in our street have their noses pressed up against their windows to see my angry father striding home. To see my sister slung across his left shoulder, frantically kicking her brown legs and working her black G-string impossibly far up her sixteen-year-old crack. To see my middle finger held up high as I go back through Mr Jessop's side gate.

He's about to heave himself off the kitchen floor when he sees me returning. He raises his arms over his head to protect himself. 'My toof. I've lost my fuckin' toof,' he moans. 'And I never even touched her. Not once.'

I tell him to shut up and calm down and stop worrying about his tooth. I tell him he is a goddamn dentist after all. Then I ask him where the rest of my sister's clothes are and he points down the corridor.

The corridor stinks. It's like some foul blend of chilli sauce and stale urine. I find Janey's stuff. There are two fresh fifties sticking out of the front pocket of her jeans. As I walk back out past Mr Jessop I don't look at him but I tell him his house stinks like Mexican cat piss. Then I walk the four doors back to my parents' house. Mrs Beveringham is still looking out her window. As usual she's trying to look unimpressed, but when I look closely I can see the slightly raised corners of her thin lips and I can guess that on the inside she's probably every bit as happy as that gnome with the missing arm.

Chapter two
The wind beneath his wings

I leave Dad and Mum and Janey shouting and go to meet Nina who's apparently on her way back from a cigarette run. Maybe she really is out of smokes. It's more likely though, that she just needed a break from Mum. I see her car about a block from my parents' house and I wave her down.

'Get ya smokes?'

She smiles and lights one up and takes a drag. 'Nup.'

In half an hour I've brought her up to speed and we're walking into our favourite beer garden, fresh beers in hand. Sure enough we find Couper sitting on his own and staring into the second half of a pint. The beer garden is full of sun and strangely empty of other people. 'Bloody good day for it,' I say. The others agree with a clink.

Couper asks how the afternoon went. I tell him it's probably still going. He shrugs his shoulders and says 'whatever' and starts telling us about how he messed with a couple of cars that were double-parked across his driveway last night. Couper lives across the road from a cinema so he's always getting cars double-parking across his driveway. Anyway, this time, he says, there's two cars blocking half the drive each. This time he doesn't bother calling the council. Instead he gets his electric drill and swaps the numberplates. God knows how long it'll be before the drivers realise their plates have been changed. Probably not until after one of them's wandered around a carpark for three hours. 'Not that those dickheads would ever pay for a parking space,' Couper says.

Couper works at a funeral home. His main task is to pick up the corpses of people who've just passed away. He's on call twenty-four hours a day for two weeks at a time. Then he has two weeks off. Apart from the pick-ups he works as a sort of death industry every-job man. He does anything that needs doing, from helping dress the corpses to answering the phones. There's nothing particularly disturbing about what he does. Just maybe sometimes about the way he does it. I arrived once to find him dumping some cremated remains along the side of his driveway. 'Couldn't fit 'em all in the urns,' he explained. When I asked whether he thought mixing them together and leaving them in his front yard was the best thing to do, he shrugged his shoulders and said he'd hose them into the gutter if it would make me feel better. When he wasn't looking I bowed my head and tried to say a quick prayer for the collective deceased at our feet. I'm not a religious nut or anything. I just reckon you've got to respect the dead. Especially when they're lying there all mixed up together next to a stack of beer cartons overflowing with empties.

Today Couper wants us to go with him to some dodgy pub to watch a talent quest. Some girl he knows is a contestant in a *Search for a Star* competition. If she wins this afternoon's grand final she'll get $2000 worth of dance tuition and the chance to record a song at Mixmasters Studios. Couper reckons she's a good chance—so much so that he's got a hundred bucks riding on her.

I tell him there's no way I'm going. I know what those talent quests are like. They're B-grade pat-each-other-on-the-back parties where genuine potential stars are rarer than blue moons. Parties organised by has-beens for a bunch of talentless try-hards who won't ever get to be has-beens because they're never even going to be is's. Couper argues 'bullshit' and that this girl Caroline can really dance and then Nina says that she reckons it'll be fun, or at least funny, and she's going, so I say 'whatever' and join them.

Nina's right. It is funny. I start smiling as soon as we walk through the door and step onto the shocking multi-coloured carpet. It's like we're walking on furry vomit. I look around me. It's the full family day out. There are proud parents and Sunday best-dressed kids everywhere. The so-called bouncers are middle-aged ladies wearing sequinned jackets. Tonight's compere is a fading local celebrity. A home shopping show host who'd be lucky to get an invitation to a community television awards after-party. I can't even remember his name. I only know that

17

he's become an expert on dog shampoo and that tonight he's genuinely proud to preside over this cavalcade of supposed up-and-coming young stars. He's as proud as the copious amounts of punch he's obviously been drinking.

Couper's chuckling at this afternoon's program. 'I'm sorry mate,' he sniggers. 'I didn't think it would be this bad. Check out the first act: "Wind Beneath my Wings", to be sung by Warren Papadopoulos, aged thirteen. I mean, shit.' He leans back against the column behind us and puts his hand to his head, laughing. 'Fucking "Wind Beneath my Wings". Oh, mate, I owe you one.'

I don't really care. I wasn't expecting much anyway. At least the beer's reasonably priced and tasting damn good. And though this place is pretty bad, it's still better than Dad's shithouse sacred front bar where I'm about as welcome as a wet track is for Pumpernickel.

'No need to be sorry, Coups,' I say, 'Should be a bit of a laugh, this.' I gulp down my beer. Couper appreciates my attempt at genuine enthusiasm. He looks at me excitedly and says he still reckons Caroline will be great. 'She's a great dancer, mate. That hundred's a sure bloody thing.'

'Sure it is, mate.'

The crowd's becoming quiet and there's reason for the hush. Less than four metres away in a sparkling red jacket and a pair of black slacks pulled up way too high, young Warren Papadopoulos is obviously nervous. He's visibly shaking in his shiny black shoes. The microphone wavers in his little hand. I almost feel sorry for the kid

18

but then I tell myself that if he's going to make it he's going to have to overcome moments like these and let his talent speak for itself.

Warren Papadopoulos stares up into the bright lights that hang above the audience and says he would like to dedicate his performance to his older brother. Apparently, Eric Papadopoulos was a champion footballer until three years ago when an on-field collision left him a paraplegic. Warren says his older brother's outlook on life has always been one hundred per cent positive in spite of all the difficulties he's faced. He says Eric is so inspiring that he himself has decided to do what he's always wanted to before it's too late: sing. 'My dear brother Eric, you are the wind beneath my wings,' Warren says, his hands clasped around the microphone.

'Yeah, yeah. Turn it up.' I look at Nina with my eyebrows raised. She rolls her eyes and pretends to stick her finger down her throat.

The backing track begins and Warren's off. And I mean he is *off*. He can't hit a single note. The poor little bastard sounds like bagpipes going through puberty. Like a cat stuck in another cat. It's the single worst performance I've ever heard in my life. I grin and look around to share a quiet laugh with someone. But my grin disappears. I can't believe what I'm seeing. The rest of the goddamn audience is transfixed.

Even though Warren is murdering this song more grotesquely than if he was deep-frying his grandmother, the crowd absolutely love him. They remain spellbound all the way through and then, unbelievably, they erupt. The applause is deafening. It's an ovation usually reserved for the likes of Pavarotti, Helfgott, Marcia Hines.

I start wondering if maybe his whole performance is a farce. Maybe it's a rort. A scam. Maybe he's just bloody well fooling everybody. After all, the little bastard can't sing to save himself, but he's a musician no doubt. He's been plucking on the audience's heartstrings like a virtuoso. Playing them for the sentimental fools they are.

'I bet he hasn't even got a paraplegic brother,' I say to Nina.

Couper hears me and says that's not the point. 'Having a brother in a wheelchair shouldn't give you an automatic right to stardom anyway,' he snorts.

I point to the young man bowing to his adoring crowd, smiling as he dodges their lobbed flowers. 'Apparently it does.'

Before he leaves the stage Warren Papadopoulos takes a final bow, throws a flower back out into the audience, pumps his young fist in the air and shouts 'I love you Eric!' It's a grand exit. He really should have been doing the finale to the whole competition instead of the opening number. He's going to be the proverbial hard act to follow. I've only pity for the next contestant. I look at the program to see that it's Couper's friend Caroline. So much for his hundred bucks. I tell Couper she'd better have a story about a brother in a wheelchair and Couper glumly says she doesn't. Biggest tragedy ever in her family was three weeks ago when her cat died after Couper put some amphetamines in its food. It flipped out and bolted across the train tracks at the wrong time. Couper says tragic though that is, a dead melted cat is no competition against a living disabled ex-football-champion brother. Nina agrees. 'Dead cats have no chance against injured humans. Anyway,' she smiles, 'that kid was so bad he was almost good. Maybe he deserves to win.'

Couper gives a chuckle of resignation. 'Nice call Kartiniski.' He looks down at the program and shakes his head in amused disbelief, muttering to himself: 'Warren Papadopoulos, eh? So fucking bad he's good.' It's a mutter that slowly evolves into a beery mantra. 'Warren Papadopoulos. So fucking bad he's good. Warren Papadopoulos. So fucking bad he's good ...'

Couper's voice is loud at the best of times but it seems especially so when the only other sound in the place is a liquored-up dog shampoo expert mumbling about the next act. The only other sound, that is, except for the whispers of disapproval about this strange bloke staring into his beer, chanting: 'Warren Papadopoulos. So fucking bad he's good. Warren Papadopoulos. So fucking bad he's good ...'

I understand that losing a bet can give rise to certain cathartic urges. But, shit Couper, there's a time and a place.

'You got a fucking problem mate?'

I look down to see an angry face in a wheelchair and

it's roughly at this point I concede that, at the very least, Warren Papadopoulos probably isn't a scam artist. That maybe he does have a paraplegic brother after all. The face in the wheelchair isn't looking at me. It's looking at Couper who's snapped out of his transcendental state and is now trying to see where that question about the problem came from. He spots the man sitting alongside me and gives him a cheeky wink. Couper's a bit pissed and I'm not sure he realises that the man he's cheekily winking at has wheels attached to his chair. That there's a high probability he's a paraplegic ex-champion-footballer called Eric Papadopoulos.

I know something unpleasant is about to happen. I know this because I know that even if Couper does realise who he's winking at it probably won't make a difference. Couper tends to treat everyone with an equal amount of disrespect. It's part of his charm.

'You got a fucking problem mate?' the man says again.

'Ah ... yes, actually,' says Couper, putting his hand thoughtfully to his chin and gazing upwards with the makings of a smile. 'Slight problem. Um ... how do I put this? That young man who was just on stage ... with his pants pulled up to his armpits—the one who sounded like a budgie being ravaged by a blue whale—you know the guy.'

The wheelchair bloke doesn't say anything. He looks frozen with anger. But I get the feeling he's not completely motionless. I get the feeling that the veins along the backs of his hands are swelling and that the pupils in his eyes are narrowing in on their target. A target that's still talking shit through an increasingly cheeky grin.

'That shiny-shoed little bastard probably just cost me a hundred bucks. And my good friend tells me it's because he's so fucking bad that he's actually good. And you know what? It's true. That little bastard probably deserves—'

'Oww!' I shout, as the bloke next to me crushes my toes with his right wheel in a frantic effort to get near Couper.

'Aaaaaaah!' yells Couper, at this nuggety former champion footballer who has literally dragged himself up Couper's torso and has a strong grip around Couper's throat and is doing his best to heave him down on to the fluffy vomit.

It's a successful tackle. 'You shut your fucking mouth!' yells Eric Papadopoulos. For a second I think Couper's trying to apologise but then I see his wicked eyes and I realise he's trying to laugh except that he can't because he can hardly breathe. Still, his wicked eyes dance. But if Couper's wicked eyes are dancing, Caroline's slender legs are not. I look up to see that she's stopped in the middle of her routine because nobody's watching her. They're all looking at Couper and Eric Papadopoulos writhing on the floor.

Michael Jackson's 'Wanna be startin' somethin'' continues to play in the background. Couper has tears forming in his eyes. Caroline has tears running down her face. She knows she's blown it big time. Stopping in the middle of a routine means certain failure. Everybody knows that. It's ridiculous but it's true. *The show must go on at all costs* the judges say. *Never let the audience know you made a mistake.* You could be having a brain haemorrhage and the judges would chide you for stopping. You could literally die, expire, pass away and you would still lose marks. After all, when you're out there performing in the real world, there's no room for mistakes, no room for death. Caroline knows this and she starts hollering into her hands as she scuttles offstage, leaving behind her the lone voice of Michael Jackson.

We manage to separate Couper and Eric. Couper's still trying to look cheeky but he can't hide his relief. He's lying on the floor rubbing the side of his head and his torso where Eric's obviously got a good few thumps in.

'Jeez mate. Take a joke.' The red welts on Couper's neck move with every word. Someone brings over Eric's wheelchair and he drags himself back in.

'Some joke mate,' he says. 'That's my little brother, you fuckin' smart-arse.'

I tell him that Couper was just mucking around and that he didn't mean any harm. 'Let us buy you a beer or two,' I say. Eric looks at me and then down at Couper and slowly nods his head. 'All right. But let's go out to the other bar. It's too hot in here.' Nina's talking to some girl who looks concerned enough to be Eric's girlfriend and I'm waiting for them to finish so I can tell them we're shifting into the front bar but I don't have to wait long because a couple of middle-aged ladies in sequinned jackets decide to stroll over and ask us all to leave.

Chapter three
The meat truck

So we're sitting around a table in the front bar. Me, Neen, Couper, Eric and Eric's girlfriend, Cass. Couper gets the first round. Five pints of Sparkling Ale. Then he gets to talking with Eric, and Neen gets to talking with Cass, and I get to drinking my beer and watching everyone talk. I listen to Couper explaining to Eric that he was just being a loudmouth because he wanted to support Caroline. That he didn't genuinely think Warren was that bad. That he didn't mean any offence, anyway. Eric counters Couper's reasonably pissed apology with a reasonably pissed apology of his own for the red welts running like sunburn up and down Couper's throat. Couper rubs his neck and laughs and says he had it coming. Then he says it's probably nothing compared with what Caroline will do to him for ruining her chances with the mid-performance scuffle. Eric apologises again and starts trying to convince Couper to go talk to her.

I get bored listening to their bonding session and start listening to the girls instead. It sounds like they work in similar jobs for similar dickheads but I'm too fuzzy to get a real grip on the conversation so I settle back into a comfortable beery haze. I can just make out the sounds of the talent quest going on in the other bar. Someone's singing 'One Perfect Day' by Little Heroes. It's my favourite eighties song. I'm almost tempted to pop next door and check it out. Almost. Neen's started rubbing me discreetly under the table. She knows how to get me going, or in this case, staying. Before too long it's like I'm not sitting in a bar anymore with my girlfriend and my best mate and two people I've only just met. It's as if I'm in bed and it's seven a.m. and I've just been woken by a certain morning blood-rush and all I want to do is lie on my back and stretch out and answer the call.

'Time for you to get the next round honey,' says Nina cheekily, withdrawing her hand, wrapping it around the bottom of her pint glass. She finishes her beer and smiles at me. 'Off you go, there's a good boy.'

I mumble something about how I'll just be a minute and I try to think of something completely boring like the periodic table. It's no good, though. The pressure's too much for me. I have to sit there looking like an idiot until Eric eventually says it may as well be his buy. Couper says he'll be back in a minute because he wants to go and find Caroline. I look around and smile stupidly and Neen smiles wickedly and Cass smiles politely and Eric wheels himself over to the bar.

I don't know how many rounds of beer we go through.

I do know though, that the punch-drinking compere's name is Bob Sanders. I know this because he comes over to our table and tells us so. Tells us that he used to host his own variety show on Channel Nine and that the boys upstairs are thinking about getting him to work on something new: a reality program about dog shows. 'Bloody dog shows, people,' he slurs, with a smile. 'It's a sure thing. And all I have to do is a few interviews. It'll be a hit.'

'Who won the talent contest?' asks Eric and Bob Sanders swears and reels around and knocks back through the swinging doors that lead to the other bar.

By the time Couper gets back we're firing on all cylinders. Caroline eventually accepted his apology but declined his offer of a lift home. I'm not surprised, seeing as he brought the meat truck. The 'meat truck' is the van he picks up dead bodies in. He shouldn't even be driving it this week because he's not on call, but try telling Couper that. 'They've got two other vans they can use,' he says. And it's true, they have. Just not any vans with advanced air-conditioning systems. 'Yeah, like the people in the back are really going to feel it anyway.'

It's well known that Couper's good for a lift home from the pub. It's also well known that there's only one spare seat up front and anyone else who wants a ride has to lie in the back in one of the cavities that have been specially installed to carry corpses. When Couper shuts the tailgate, it's pitch black in there. It's pretty unsettling.

At least it was the last time I got a ride. Couper was dropping me and Nina home when he got a call to pick up a corpse. Of course, I couldn't hear anything while I was lying there in the back in the dark. The first I heard about the pick-up was when he opened the tailgate and whispered for me to shut up. Then he slid a goddamn dead body along the level above me and slammed the tailgate shut. It probably only took about twenty minutes to get home but when I got there my face had turned white. I nearly punched Couper out when he eventually opened that tailgate again but Nina was laughing so hard that I found myself starting to laugh as well. My face stayed white for a while longer though. And even now, while I can forgive Couper for my ride with death, I'll never forget.

At some point Eric's brother Warren comes over with his parents and his first-place trophy and we all slap him on the back and tell him he deserved to win and that he'll go far and that we agree his brother Eric is one helluva guy. I think I start asking him whether he's going to stick that trophy on a mantelpiece for the rest of his life like my dad's done with his silver medallion but I only get a few words out before Nina squeezes my kneecap so hard I temporarily lose the ability to speak. Couper offers Warren a glass of vodka and soda but Mrs Papadopoulos overhears and suddenly tells us they have to be going and thanks us for coming along and showing our support. Then Bob Sanders is upon us again and he's halfway through telling Mr Papadopoulos about his idea for a dog show that he's been running past the boys upstairs when Mr Papadopoulos interrupts and says they really have to be going and that Bob Sanders did a great job of hosting the night and thank you very much and good luck with the dog show but they really have to be going.

So Bob sits down with us and we keep drinking until they shut the bar. Then we decide to go back to Couper's house for a couple more. Couper'll drive us there. He's only parked two blocks away. I never thought I'd ride in the meat truck again but tonight I'm so pissed that I'll take whatever lift's going. Somehow Bob Sanders gets the front seat which means the other four of us have to ride in the two corpse compartments. Me and Couper help Eric up to the top one and Cass climbs in after him. Couper sticks the wheelchair in the storage gap behind the passenger seat while I climb into the lower compartment and snuggle up to Neen. Then the tailgate slams shut and pretty shortly we hear the engine revving and then we're off. Before we even turn the first corner I reach down to drag Nina's knickers off. There's no noise from above so I assume Eric and Cass pretty much have their own thing going on. I start hoping Couper doesn't get the idea of pulling over and running around to catch us in the act. I wouldn't put it past him, but he's talking to Bob Sanders so his deviant mind is hopefully already occupied—even if it's only in the same sort of way a public toilet can be.

Nina's turned over and she's tugging on my hard-ish cock and trying to put me inside her. I lie back and shut my eyes and try to concentrate on not losing what erection I've got because let's face it, I've had a few beers. I'll be damned though, if my mind doesn't keep coming up with all the bloody elements of the periodic table. I'm afraid mental control is probably not the best thing to rely on right now. The best thing is for me to be inside Nina. And then suddenly I am. And I hold up her dress and cling to her hips. Then I try to lean forward and kiss the back of her neck but her hair's everywhere and I'm starting to lose concentration so I just lean back against the side of the meat truck and let her pump against me.

Then I start hearing some unfamiliar high-pitched little moans. Ones that I haven't heard Nina make. It takes me a good three seconds to realise the divider's creaking above us and the moans are Cass's. At least, I hope they are. If they're Eric's, then chances are there'll be another fight on as soon as we get out of this bloody van.

Quite frankly when you're having drunken sex at four in the morning in the back of a corpse truck you need everything you can get to help the excitement factor. So my hands cling to Nina's hips and my ears cling to Cass's moans and pretty soon it all comes together, even if we don't. And then me and Neen lie there listening to the meat truck engine purring and listening to Cass sort of purring, and reassuring each other with gentle finger strokes that things are now as good as they ever were and that they will continue to be so.

There are no screeching brakes. The only sounds I hear are the crunching of metal and the crashing of broken glass and the thumps of our own heads. Then a cacophony of fucks and shits. It's damn scary in the pitch black so I kick against the back tailgate until Couper opens it up. He looks freaked out. 'Get out. Quick,' he says. 'We've got to get the fuck out of here.'

He doesn't need to tell us twice. Eric's already dragged himself out and he's hanging off the top of the tailgate, naked from the waist down. 'Get us the fucking chair!'

I'm still trying to do up my pants as I bolt around the side of the van to grab his wheels. I see Bob Sanders lurching off down the street and I yell out to him but he either doesn't hear me or pretends not to. Cass and Nina are out and adjusting their clothes and rubbing their heads and looking shocked. 'Hurry up!' yells Couper and pretty soon we're legging and wheeling it up the street as fast as we can and the meat truck's revs are fading in the distance, along with a concussed television personality.

We're only about four blocks from Couper's house and so we're on his front porch in a matter of minutes. Everyone's in that weird place somewhere between being too drunk to be shocked and too shocked to be drunk. We don't even go inside. We just stand there on the porch. I'm smoking a cigarette and wondering if the buzzing in my ears is the sound of the meat truck still revving or just a buzzing in my ears. Then Nina interrupts the buzzing. 'What the hell happened Couper?'

Couper says he thinks he hit a parked car on the side of the road. He must be really drunk tonight. 'Going to bed,' he says and reaches for his keys but then he realises that he's left them in the van. And his spares aren't under the mat like they're supposed to be. He flips the doormat back over and looks at me. 'You take my spares? Where are my keys for fuck's sake?'

I notice a couple of cops coming up the driveway. 'Coups,' I say. 'I think we're screwed.'

I'm not entirely right. It's only Couper who's screwed in the end.

As the cops get closer, I realise that I know one of them. Ben McPhenton. Went to high school with him. He was a couple of years below me. He still looks young. Too young to be a copper anyway.

'Hey, Ben.'

He doesn't recognise me at first. Then he calls me by my last name. 'Millevic,' he nods, without smiling. The other cop raises her eyebrows. Ben looks at her as if to say he can't help who he went to high school with. I can tell he's embarrassed to know me. Right now I don't blame him. I mean it's not like we've just bumped into each other at a nominee's briefing for Young Australian of the Year. To be honest, I'm a little embarrassed myself. Standing here with my fly open, on a porch with four other pissheads, one of whom, my best mate, just drove his work van fair up the arse of a parked car. I look at Ben McPhenton. He looks immaculate. He also looks bored, tired and irritated. I think he might have more important things to do than deal with people like us.

'So what're you doing these days Millevic?' he asks, in a tone of voice that suggests he doesn't give a fuck what I'm doing these days.

I shrug. 'Uh ... I used to go to uni,' I say.

He's not even listening. He's looking at Couper. 'Right,' he says. 'These the keys you're looking for?' He holds up Couper's keys. He must have taken them from the van.

Suddenly Couper's like a school kid who's been caught cheating in front of the whole class. He's got everyone looking at him and so he refuses to lose face. Refuses to make excuses or apologise. Refuses to be anything but a smart-arse. He gives a wink and a smile. 'You got me, cunt-stable Benjamin. I'm the one you want.' And then he's confessing to being the driver of the smashed up van. But it's a confession with a Couper twist. 'I was only driving three-quarters of that van,' he says. 'I wasn't driving the bit that crashed. I want that stricken from my record, cunt-stable. D'ya hear me? Stricken from my record!'

He's rambling like an idiot. The two young constables look at one another for a few moments as if to non-verbally discuss the best plan of action. Couper grows impatient and cheekily tips Ben McPhenton's hat off. 'Did you hear me cunt-stable?'

34

Non-verbal discussion over. Four arms upon Couper and one stern voice telling him, 'All right, buddy, that's enough. You're coming with us.'

They've got him by the arms and they're encouraging him to join them for a walk down the driveway. Couper wisely decides resistance is useless and then, less wisely, decides to begin singing into Ben McPhenton's ear: *'Did you ever know that you're my heroooooooooooo? You're everything I would like to beeeeeeeeeeee.'*

They won't be doing him any favours when they get him back to the station. Can't say I blame them. Couper makes Warren Papadopoulos sound like a fucking angel.

Chapter four
Heady days indeed

I wake up before Nina, so I lie there and watch her sleep for a while. She's got black bags under her closed eyes. It's no wonder she looks tired even though she's asleep. After the cops took Couper away last night we hit the town again. Eric and Cass caught a cab home. They were pretty shaken up. At five o'clock this morning it was just me and Nina sitting in a dodgy bar listening to dodgy music and drinking dodgy vodka and oranges. Just like we did on our first date, only then I was wearing a nicer t-shirt, I think.

I'm as hungover as I've ever been. I get up to take a crap. It's a hot day and the bathroom's like an oven. I sit there straining and sweating and thinking about the situation yesterday with Janey and Mr Jessop. I can't believe the dirty bastard was jerking off in his kitchen like that. Over my goddamn sixteen-year-old sister. I manage a resigned laugh. Hell, of course I believe it. I shouldn't even be surprised. Nothing should surprise me after what happened with Aaron.

Aaron used to be a family friend of sorts. He got to know my parents while he was here for a year as an exchange lecturer from Canada and I ended up cleaning his pool for him all summer. He paid me ten bucks an hour. Not a bad wage for a seventeen-year-old who was still at school. And not a bad wage for a thirty-six-year-old to pay. At least once a week, Aaron used to sit by the pool with a cold beer and watch me catch a tan and as many floating leaves as I could.

A couple of weeks before he was due to return to Canada, Aaron asked me if I wanted to join him and two of his lady friends for a few beers on a Saturday night. I was stoked. At seventeen I was more used to getting drunk with my mates than with a grown man and two real life ladies. I felt sophisticated. Adult, even. 'I'll be there,' I said. There was just one problem. Being somewhat baby-faced, I had trouble buying alcohol.

'No problem,' Aaron said. 'I'll pick up the booze. Just maybe don't tell your mother.'

So the next Saturday night it was on. There were four of us. Aaron from Canada. Sophie and Trudy from Sydney and me fresh from the Saturday lunch shift at the Tin Pan Café. With the pool cleaning, I was technically working two jobs. Heady days indeed. The girls congratulated me on how clean the pool looked. They'd been using it all day. Aaron said I was a bloody magician and Sophie said a good-looking one at that. So I started feeling good straight away and got a beer and joined them on the lounge suite.

We drank fast and talked fast as the afternoon flew by. I didn't even notice when the sun went down. I lost all track of time. The only things that made sense were the beer which tasted good and Sophie's brown shoulders which looked great.

Then I noticed Sophie had stretched her legs out and was asking whether I minded if she rested them on my thighs. Aaron had his arm around Trudy and he gave a wink and said something to Sophie like 'I'm sure he doesn't mind at all.' Trudy polished off her drink and ducked into the kitchen. I looked down at Sophie's legs. They were very brown, which somehow made them look less thick than they were. She kicked her sandals off and brought her legs to my lap. I watched her feet, which were also brown, tapping against each other. They were tapping pretty close to my groin. I looked at her face and she was smiling at me. I smiled back and reached over to grab my beer but it'd been replaced with a scotch and coke.

'Would you like another drink as well, my dear?' Aaron asked Sophie. She said she would so he brought her one and went back into the kitchen where Trudy was, leaving me and Sophie on the couch.

I was getting pretty pissed and so my conversation wasn't exactly sharp, but it didn't seem to need to be. We weren't saying much. Just sitting there lightly holding hands and drinking. After a while, without even thinking, I shifted Sophie's feet so they rested directly on my groin and couldn't believe my luck when she started playfully rubbing her heels against me.

Then we heard a raised voice in the other room. 'Aaron! Stop it!' Sophie quickly took her legs away and got up and I followed her to the kitchen where I was more than a little surprised to see Trudy standing naked from the waist up. She had a huge dark purple birthmark that covered more than half her torso, including most of one of her large breasts. We walked in just as Aaron was telling Trudy he didn't mind.

'But I do.' Her voice was angry and definite. 'You're being a sleaze. Now give me back my top.' Aaron looked around and saw Sophie and me and immediately replaced his beady-eyed eagerness with a big friendly smile and handed Trudy back her top. 'Thank you,' she said as she snatched it from his hands. 'Now will you please leave me alone?'

Aaron backed away, saying he didn't mean anything by anything. Sophie squeezed my hand and gave me a look and went to talk to Trudy.

Aaron and I went back out to the billiards room for a game. About half an hour later Sophie popped her head in to say Trudy had crashed on the couch and that she was going to do the same. Aaron told her she could sleep in his double bed if she liked and that he'd be happy to sleep in the spare room.

Sophie said, 'Okay then, but you'd better make sure you do,' and went off to his bedroom. She gave me kind of a look before she left. As soon as she'd gone, Aaron asked me what I was waiting for.

'For you to have your shot.'

'Not the game—Sophie. She wants you. I could see it in her eyes.'

'Don't be stupid.'

'Go up to her room,' he said. 'Go on.' Then he smiled wickedly. 'She wants you *bad*.'

I thought about it. Maybe he was right. Maybe she did want me. But I still had my doubts. And I didn't want to make Sophie angry like Aaron had made Trudy. 'What if she doesn't? I'm just going to look like a dick if I go up there and try something.'

'Look, just go up and say you need to borrow a pair of my boxer shorts. If she doesn't want you there, you'll know and you can leave right away. You can't lose.' Then he poured me a double scotch. 'Here. Get this into you.'

I was drunk enough already but I took the scotch and sculled it down and nodded and started making my way to Aaron's bedroom, where I knew a twenty-eight-year-old woman from Sydney with great shoulders and thick brown legs had gone to bed. I didn't know whether she was expecting me. All I knew was that I hadn't felt a female breast since I was thirteen, and to be honest, it was much more of a nipple than a breast. That was the extent of my preparation for that night. Forty fumbling seconds under a blanket at a teenage party with a girl who happened to be the only kid in my class going through puberty slower than I was.

I opened the door. The bedroom lights were off.

'Oh fuck off Aaron—'

I fumbled with the switch.

'Oh. It's you.'

She was lying on her back under the quilt. She'd taken her hair down. She looked as vulnerable as I felt.

'I just came up to get some boxer shorts,' I said. 'Do you know where they are?' Then I sat down on the bed and leant over to go through Aaron's drawers. I was beginning to feel like this was a stupid idea. I felt like I'd just reached the top of a ten-metre diving board and now I wanted to go back down the ladder. I had one thing on my mind and that was to get a pair of boxer shorts and get out. But Sophie was suddenly looking more and more like she wanted to push me off the springboard.

'Shut the door.'

Like a robot I leant over and pushed it shut. She smiled cheekily. 'What do you need boxer shorts for?' She edged nearer and poked me in the ribs. 'Eh?' She poked me again. I winced. She gave a cheeky grin. 'Are you ticklish?'

My response was automatic. 'Are you?'

'No.'

'We'll see about that.' I leant over to give her a good tickling. Immediately she thrashed about squealing and in the process she somehow threw the quilt off. Suddenly, lying there right in front of me was the first naked woman

I'd ever seen. She had a frighteningly big mound of hair between her legs which I could hardly take my eyes off. Her breasts were much smaller than I thought breasts normally were and her thick thighs sprouted from much thicker, rounder hips. She had a small ball of a stomach and thin arms and big brown eyes. Her face was the last thing I looked at. She'd stopped looking cheeky. 'Take off your clothes,' she said. And I did.

I lay on top of her and we kissed and then I tried to stick my finger inside her pussy but she was awfully tight. She seemed to suddenly tense right up and she told me to slow down a bit. Then she told me that she'd only done this once before when she was about fifteen and that she hadn't enjoyed it at all so I was her first for a long, long time. And she was only doing it with me because she had a funny feeling she could trust me. She said she usually didn't trust men. Not after what happened the last time.

I didn't ask her what happened but I told her that I wasn't a man yet, so she had nothing to worry about. She laughed at that and relaxed a bit. I asked her whether I could look at her properly. She slowly opened her legs and I lowered my face so that my chin brushed across that thick mound of pubic hair and then I was looking right at her vagina. It looked strange. Red. I could feel some sort of heat near my lips. I tried again to stick my finger in there but I couldn't force it. 'Hang on,' she said and licked her own fingers and rubbed the saliva around her slit. She tried to put her fingers in but even *she* couldn't. She was too dry and hot and tight. I tried to lick it but I didn't know what to do and whatever I was doing didn't appear to be working. All I could feel on my tongue was heat and the texture of tiny bumps. Then her arms reached down to pull me up and she told me just to kiss her.

So I started kissing her again and I started rubbing myself against her and she rubbed back against me and we did this for a while and then I looked up and I saw Aaron leaning in the door with a weird half-smile on his face. I didn't know how long he'd been there. I was seventeen and shit-faced, so to me there was nothing particularly strange about Aaron watching me rub against a woman in his bed. I was about to say hi but he put his finger to his lips, leant over and put a condom on the bedside table and then quietly closed the door. I reached over and grabbed the condom but I couldn't put it on and she couldn't put it on me, even though we tried for ages. It was frustrating. We both wanted to fuck so badly. Just not *this* badly.

In the end we forgot the condom and she just sort of forced my hard-on halfway inside her pussy which was still so dry and raw and tight it actually hurt my cock. Still, I kept trying to thrust while Sophie lay there frozen except for her thin arms which clung around my back and somehow eventually I dribbled out some come. And then I was a man and I turned and flopped my drunken head on the mattress just in time to see our bedroom door quietly shutting again.

Sophie and Trudy were already on their plane back to Sydney when I woke up. I lay in Aaron's bed for a while, hungover as a dog, thinking about Sophie's giant mound of pubic hair. Perhaps all girls were like that, I thought. I thought about how red and raw her pussy was and about how I couldn't put my condom on and how I never even got my whole dick inside her. But I did come, I told myself, and that was the main thing wasn't it? I wasn't a virgin anymore.

And this is what I told Aaron the following Saturday night. He'd invited me over again, for a boys' night, he said. He had a bottle of scotch, a bottle of vodka and a bottle of gin, but we started off with a few beers around the swimming pool. He'd even cleaned it himself that day. 'Just to say thanks for all the work this year,' he told me.

I was feeling pretty good as I lay there in the sun. The awkwardness of my first intercourse didn't seem so bad a week later. I'd almost managed to convince myself it was somewhat of a success. I lay back and soaked up the sun and soaked up the beer until there was no more sun and no more beer and Aaron suggested we go into the lounge to have a few scotches. When we were comfortably sprawled he told me: 'You're a dog.'

'A dog?'

'You're the man. Going in and giving it to Sophie like

that. Good on you.' Aaron raised his glass to me. I smiled and drank some more.

'Better luck than me anyway,' he said.

'Yeah, what happened there? Did you get a bit?' I was trying to sound like the dog I supposedly was. Aaron said he got a bit. But not enough. Said that Trudy was embarrassed about her birthmark and that she wasn't feeling that great anyway.

'Too bad,' I said. 'I guess I just got lucky and picked the right one.'

'I guess so,' smiled Aaron.

So we talked some more and Aaron wanted to know how I felt about not being a virgin anymore.

'Just kind of good, I guess,' I said. I didn't really know how I felt. I had some more scotch and I asked him what he was going to do when he got back to Canada and he said he didn't really know, he just wanted to find a good woman to fuck like a rabbit for a while. I said 'yeah' and we kept talking about fucking women like rabbits even though I was making most of my stuff up or guessing. We had a few more scotches and I started telling him about my job at the Tin Pan Café and how I wanted to quit and he said if I ever saved up the money I could come and stay with him in Canada and we could go and paint the town red. 'Go out to clubs and even fuck the girls in the toilets,' he said. Then he asked me if I'd ever had a blow job from a strange girl in the toilet and I said I hadn't and he said 'you don't know what you're missing.'

I knocked back my glass of scotch and closed my eyes and started thinking about getting a blow job in the toilet. Any sort of blow job, actually. I'd never had one. Sophie hadn't given me one the week before. She'd just lain there stiff as a post except for her arms. 'Yeah, I'd really like a blow job from a hot chick,' I said.

'Nothing better,' said Aaron and poured me a glass of vodka because we'd finished the scotch.

So we kept drinking and we kept talking and for some reason, Aaron kept steering every conversation back to sex. I didn't mind though because apart from the fact that I'd gotten laid last week with a twenty-eight-year-old chick from Sydney, I was more drunk on scotch, vodka, and now gin, than I'd ever been and I didn't mind having a bit of a brag and listening to a few of Aaron's brags. But the more pissed I got, the less I wanted to brag and the more I wanted to do it again. 'I wish Sophie was here,' I said, as I staggered off to the billiards room. 'I'd give her a real pounding this time.'

Aaron followed me, laughing. 'I bet you would.'

'Don't you wish Trudy was here? So you could have another crack at those massive tits?'

'Mate, she had areolas the size of dinner plates didn't she?'

'Yeah.' Wow, I thought: areolas. I've never heard tits called that before. And then I thought: isn't Aaron standing a bit close?

I held out a pool cue and backed away a little. 'Do you feel like a game of pool?'

Aaron took the cue out of my hands and placed it on the table. 'Maybe later,' he said. 'But do you know what? Do you know what I really feel like now? With all this talk all night, I mean, Christ.' He looked up at the ceiling and held his hands out. 'I just feel like sex,' he smiled, and shook his head. I knew what he meant. I was so wishing Sophie was there.

'Me too,' I laughed. 'Me too.'

'I really feel like sex,' said Aaron again and touched me gently on the arm.

'Me too,' I said again. And I think we just stood there for a moment or two. Then somehow both his arms were around me and I felt myself dropping down to the carpet with him and then I felt his tongue inside my mouth. It felt a lot different to Sophie's tongue. Bigger. Thicker. Stronger. I didn't know if I liked it or not. I was too drunk to know anything except that I felt like sex and so I licked that tongue and kissed and sucked his lips and ignored the grip of the hand on my arse.

Then I looked down and saw my first erect male penis that was not my own. It was much bigger than mine and surrounded by a thick bush of red pubic hair. It was a thirty-six-year-old penis. It looked like a big red hairy muppet. I almost expected to hear 'Mana-Mana' playing in the background and see Kermit bobbing into the room, microphone in hand. But the only thing I heard was Aaron's groans and the only thing bobbing in that room was my head and the thing in my hand wasn't a microphone. I was jerking and sucking and licking like there was no tomorrow and in some ways there wasn't one. Aaron's voice was guiding me with instructions: 'not so fast, not so hard.' I couldn't hear his voice well because his palms were covering my ears as he gripped my head. I was reminded of school days when we used to watch the braver thirteen-year-old couples kiss each other in a massive grotto of pine trees. I was reminded of the day that Petra van Winkelreid was so inexperienced at tongue kissing that she nearly swallowed Brett Rosevear's whole head in a particularly energetic pash. She ended up biting his lip so hard it bled. I felt like Petra van Winkelreid lying on that carpet. I didn't know what I was supposed to be doing. Schoolyard whispers had always told me that this was something that only 'faggots' did. Not seventeen-year-old schoolboys and thirty-six-year-old family friends.

But we were doing it.

Aaron led me into the bedroom and told me to lay down on my back and then he knelt over me facing the other way and held his dick over my face so I had to lift my head to lick it. Then he started kissing and sucking on mine. But I couldn't get hard. I was as limp as Sophie was tight. I could feel his unshaven prickle against my skin and it scratched. I asked him to have a shave and followed him into the bathroom where he shaved and I got on my knees and continued to give my best attempt at a blow job and out of the corner of my eye I could see the toilet.

When he'd finished shaving we went back into the bedroom and resumed our position on the bed. Aaron lay next to me and played with my dick. Then he got me to lie on top of him and rub against him while he kissed me. He seemed to enjoy that the most. Myself, I didn't really know whether I enjoyed it or not. I was so goddamn drunk. All I knew was that every time I saw Aaron's face I just had to look somewhere else. And after a while, when he kept sticking his tongue down the back of my throat, I started trying to turn my head. Eventually I just lay there and let him hold me to him. Until he suggested that we get dressed and go and have another drink.

'But you haven't blown your load,' I said. 'Don't you want to blow your load?'

Aaron smiled and said, 'No, it's okay.'

So I went out of the bedroom and I found my clothes and got dressed and went into the lounge room where he was waiting for me on the couch, dressed in a fresh Hawaiian shirt and pants and holding out a gin and tonic. He was wearing a big friendly smile and looked almost like he did when my parents first introduced me to him. Like a red-haired Mr Brady. We had another drink and we didn't say much and then we went to sleep in separate beds. I woke up at about five in the morning and left without waking him and I never saw him again. And I've never talked to anyone about him but Neen.

I get off the toilet and wipe my arse and flush and

kneel down for a spew. I've got bile rising in my throat. I must have smoked too many cigarettes last night. I breathe in the cistern atmosphere and heave and retch so hard that when I get up and look in the bathroom mirror I see that I've burst a blood vessel in my eyeball. I wash my face and start to clean my teeth and wonder whether Couper's in a jail cell somewhere.

Chapter five
Runaways

The first thing I do after I clean my teeth is ring Janey to
see how she is. Mum answers the phone. She sounds upset.
I can always tell when Mum's upset because she speaks
in an unusually loud monotone, like a hard-of-hearing
dalek. She says, 'JANEY RAN AWAY YESTERDAY AND
APPARENTLY YOUR FATHER AND I CAN GO AND FUCK
OURSELVES.'

I'm surprised to hear my mum use such language,
even if she is only repeating it. Even if she is upset. It's
not the only thing I'm surprised about either. I can't quite
believe Janey hasn't turned up at my house. I always
assumed if she ever ran away from them, she'd run to me.

I wonder where she's gone. It wouldn't be somewhere
obvious like one of her schoolfriends' houses. She's savvy
enough to know that their parents would give her up
straight away. I hope she hasn't slept out in the parklands
or something. I knew a girl in primary school who did that
when she ran away from home. Her name was Christine
Spence and she was a pretty smart kid. Too damn smart,

I would have thought, to run away and sleep on a park bench at the age of eleven. The last reported sighting of Christine Spence was of her in a white parka and floral dress sitting on a swing in the parklands. Some people reckoned she made a clean break. I suppose it's possible. Other people said they didn't even want to guess what happened to her. I'm one of those people. And I wouldn't want to guess what had happened to Janey if I never saw her again either. But I don't tell Mum that. I just tell her not to worry and that I'll call her again later.

I run back to the bedroom and take a flying leap into bed. Neen pretends she's still asleep but I can tell she's trying not to smile. I blow cool ticklish air inside her ear until she can't hold a straight face any longer. She wriggles under the doona squealing and then emerges with her eyes shut and her arms held out for a hug and her lips puckered for a kiss. I snuggle up against her and plant a quick one. Crikey. She's got some serious morning-after breath. I don't care how much I love her. I can't kiss a mouth like that more than once.

'Um ... honey, I think you need to clean your teeth.'

'You can talk, spewboy.'

Bloody Neen doesn't miss a thing. I roll on to my back. 'Yeah, yeah, all right. I had a spew. But I cleaned my teeth after.'

'Okay, okay.' She mock sighs and then bounds out of bed like a big happy dog and she's back almost straight away. She kneels over me on her hands and knees and breathes some generic brand of freshmint over my face. 'All right now, Mr Fusspot?' Then she gives me one of her excellent kisses and lays down on top of me. Through a mouthful of her hair I tell her about Janey doing a runner. Neen suggests we go out looking for her. At least—that's what Neen's mouth suggests. Neen's hand is currently suggesting something else. And I'm all ears.

If sexual intercourse was an official national sport, then me and Neen would be what you call a couple of C-grade amateurs. That's not to say we can't play. It's just that our main motivation is our love of the game. Whatever the weather, however bad the injuries, we just go out there and give it a bash. Sometimes one of us plays a shit game, sometimes we both do. Sometimes we both play a blinder. Either way, we go back and coach ourselves and each other and look forward to the next match. We're a couple of pot-bellied, cuddly-arsed lovers. We believe all that matters is that you enjoy making an effort. Admittedly, it's lucky we both believe this. If only one of us did, our relationship would be a tragedy waiting to happen.

It's a fairly short game this morning and I'm not exactly best on ground. In twenty minutes we're warming up the car. Looking for my runaway sister seems like a good idea until we actually pull out of the driveway. 'Now where?' says Neen. We sit there for a few minutes trying to think. Then I tell Nina about Christine Spence and so we go and check the parklands.

It's cold out. We stand near the playground and shiver and gaze around uselessly for a while. Then I see a car pull up on the other side of the playground. It's my dad in his purple Kingswood. He must have remembered Christine Spence as well. Probably hoping his little girl's sitting on a swing somewhere telling herself she's right. Just like he'll probably end up doing on a bar stool. I'm not much up for a conversation with the old man right now, so before he sees us, me and Neen turn around and go back to the car.

We waste another hour driving around before we go home. When we get there I head for the couch. Neen tells me not to get too comfortable, she wants me to think about doing some vacuuming. Damn. And there I was thinking about how much I'd like a cold beer. Some people might even say I deserve one. It's been a full-on twenty-four hours. I get up to check the fridge. There's only one long-neck of Melbourne Bitter left, but the good news is that Neen doesn't feel like a beer yet so I get it all to myself. Great. Something to take the edge off while I suck up dust.

I do most of the housework around our place and Neen pays most of our living costs. It's an agreement we made after it became apparent that my dole money wasn't exactly cutting it when it came to paying the bills. Neen reckons people should do what they're able to at the time. She's making enough money to see us right for now, she reckons. But she doesn't have a lot of spare time. And seeing as I do, she said, it makes sense that

I do something useful with it. So began my life as Vacuum Boy.

The bedroom needs a going over, but first things first. I take my beer out on the porch, find my cigarettes and light one up. Then I remember that I only just finished coughing up a huge ball of mucus two hours ago. That I only just finished bursting a blood vessel in my eye. I can feel my first drag threatening to wake the remaining bile slumbering against the walls of my oesophagus. I don't really feel like another coughing fit so I butt out what is nearly a whole cigarette and wash out my stale mouth with a big gulp of Melbourne and sit and listen to distant traffic. I listen until I've all but finished that longneck of beer. Then I go inside to our bedroom. It smells. I open the window to let some air in.

Nina comes in as I start up the vacuum cleaner. 'Christ, this room stinks.'

'It's probably just the dirty clothes basket,' I say. And then I think—bugger.

'Will you do the washing today then?'

I pretend not to hear her over the vacuum cleaner and she has to ask me again before I grunt a yes. I was going to do it anyway, just probably tomorrow. I ask how her stomach is today. She pretends not to hear over the vacuum cleaner and so I have to ask again before she tells me she's fine.

Neen gets a bad stomach now and then. Well, more often than not. It used to be worse before she went on the pill, but now she reckons that it's coming back nearly as bad as it ever was. I reckon she should go see a doctor but she says it's just her normal period pain, and she just gets on with things. Except when she physically can't. Like when she has to take the day off work. Or sometimes when sex hurts too much and we have to stop.

The first time that happened I suggested that maybe my dick was a bit big for her. Nina eventually managed to stop laughing long enough to tell me not to worry. Apparently I wasn't the problem. But she couldn't tell me what was, and we still haven't worked it out. Whenever I bring it up she says the best way I can help her is to just shut up about it. And to give her good cuddles.

When I've finished vacuuming, I get our dirty clothes and put them in the machine. I figure I'll walk down and pick up some beer while they're washing. I don't have to walk, I could borrow Neen's car. But I won't. My head's a hungover blur and I'm feeling shaky as shit. It was touch and go whether I should have even been operating a vacuum cleaner. There's no way I'm putting myself in control of anything that moves at sixty kilometres an hour.

When I get back with the beer we sit outside with a cold one each and listen to the washing machine do its stuff. We end up sitting there for a couple of hours and we have a few more beers and even a few cigarettes, and though I'm not completely enjoying them, I'm well past the point of feeling like I'm going to spew again. We're back in bed before midnight. Nina has to start work at the service station at midday tomorrow. It's a shithouse job for a girl who's got a university degree, but that's the way things are these days. Anyway, she couldn't give a shit about her job. She only gives a shit about me and her dad. Considering her dad's dead that only really leaves me. Me who waits in the car for her. Me who worries about her but shuts up about it and gives good cuddles. Me who's knackered from beer and cigarettes and vacuuming and who's lying quietly next to her in bed, wondering just where the hell my little sister could be.

Chapter six
Mick the prick

The next night I'm sitting on the couch with a beer and a smoke when Nina gets home from work at nine o'clock. She looks worn out. I offer her a beer but she doesn't want anything to drink. She just wants to go to bed. I tell her I'm staying up for a bit and she tells me not to drink heaps and then fart all night because she doesn't want to wake up at four in the morning and have to air the room out yet again. I nod and keep my mouth shut because I can tell she's not in the greatest of moods. I don't blame her. She's been working all day and her boss is a complete prick.

We call him Mick the prick. Nina's been working at one of his new service stations. It's out in the sticks, in an area where there's some serious unemployment. The service station's been up and running for about three months but Mick still hasn't got the EFTPOS system sorted out properly yet. So Nina has to do all the card transactions manually—swipe the plastic and then hand-write all the details in. This means, of course, that she can't tell whether a customer has got enough money in their account or not. A lot of the people who live out that way don't have much money at all. And it didn't take them long to work out that they could get away with overdrawing their accounts.

Now the place is going ballistic. There are queues that stay twenty people long for eight hours at a time. Everyone lining up with their plastic cards. No one's buying petrol though. They're buying cartons of cigarettes, weeks' worth of groceries and just about anything else they can see. Mick the prick isn't worried that they're spending money they don't have. He knows he'll get paid in the end. In fact Nina reckons he's deliberately delaying the EFTPOS machine installations so he can lead these folks into as much debt as possible. They know he's doing it and they don't care. They must think they'll never have to pay. Maybe they think the banks will. In a fake show of responsibility Mick the prick's imposed a purchase limit of a hundred dollars per person per day. He ignores the fact that some kid's been stocking up on a carton and a half of cigarettes every day for ten weeks straight. Nina's tried complaining to Mick the prick and she's even tried reasoning with the customers, but no one listens. Greed and necessity prevail.

After writing out those transaction details for eight hours straight, day after day, week after week, Neen's hands have started to ache with a constant dull arthritic throb. And after spending three months looking down the daily barrel of a twenty-person queue, Nina's started seeing her job and her boss in the worst light possible. And it's never a big step from hating your boss to stealing from him. For the last month or so, Neen's been lifting about a hundred bucks a week from the till. 'Sore fingers fund' she calls it. She can call it whatever she wants. She bloody well deserves it. Especially when she's coming home looking as buggered as she does tonight.

As soon as she goes into the bedroom and shuts the door, the phone rings. It's Couper. I knew he'd surface eventually. He sounds unusually serious. I tell him to lob over for a couple of bevvies and he says okay and he's gonna bring a mate if it's all right. I say fine. Just that we can't be too loud cos Neen's knackered and she's gotta work again tomorrow. 'No worries,' he says. He's over in fifteen minutes, and his 'mate' is Janey.

'Hi bro,' she says, as if she's just popped in for a chat—which I guess is what she's done, only she's been missing for a couple of days.

'Hi Janey.'

I don't know what else to say yet so I go into the kitchen and I get a beer for Couper and come back and I ask him how things went with the cops. He can't remember much. Just riding in the back of the car and going to the station-house to sign a few forms. Then he woke up yesterday in a cell. When they let him go, he went home to find Janey sitting on his couch watching the afternoon soapies and eating the last of his cheese and onion chips. She'd let herself in with the spare keys.

Now I know what to say. 'So that's where they bloody well went.'

'Can I have a beer please Mico?'

I tell Janey I didn't know she liked beer. Or cheese and onion chips for that matter. She shrugs. I tell her I certainly didn't think she knew where Couper lived. She tells me she's gone to a couple of his parties. That she's even danced with me at one of them. 'Yeah right,' I say, as I head to the kitchen to get her a stubbie. 'As if I'd remember one of Couper's parties.' I look back at Couper and he shrugs too.

The other night he blew 0.196. He'll have to go to court in a couple of months and he's pretty much guaranteed to lose his licence. He's also pretty much guaranteed to lose his job. The funeral parlour don't know about the accident yet. Apparently the cops haven't got around to telling them. Couper's going in to fess up tomorrow. I'd love to tell the guy everything's going to be okay but I can't. So I hand Janey her beer and put my hand on Couper's shoulder and tell him, 'Who gives a shit anyway.'

Couper's voice replies, 'Yeah, who gives a shit,' but his face says maybe something else.

Janey, on the other hand, is looking pretty damn relaxed. She says she went to Couper's house because she thought Mum and Dad would look for her at my place.

'They didn't. They didn't even call to tell me you'd gone.'

She looks surprised at this. I have to say that I'm a little surprised too. I mean, considering my apparent history as an anti-authoritarian and all, surely they'd expect me to have a goddamn network of safe-houses scattered throughout the city or something.

'I think you should give them a call,' I say. 'It's the least you can do.' I tell Janey she can't blame them for being a little freaked out after what happened at Mr Jessop's.

'Piss off Mico. I was just playing tennis.'

'Oh, come on Janey. You know what Jessop was doing, for fuck's sake.'

'Like I said: I was just playing tennis.' She pauses and then rolls her eyes. 'Oh look, he never even touched me y'know? If that dirty bastard wants to give me a hundred bucks so he can get his rocks off, then so fuckin' what?' She smiles suddenly. 'Anyway, I needed to practise my backhand.'

'Oh yeah, very fuckin' funny. Until something happens that you weren't expecting. What if—'

'Look, get off my fuckin' case will ya? Christ, what's next? Some good chocca rules for success?'

It's a cheap shot but she's got a point. Time to change the subject. I notice that she hasn't opened her beer yet.

'So are you gonna drink that or not?'

She shakes her head and says she doesn't really feel like it after all and that maybe she and Couper should go.

'But you just got here.'

'Yeah, I know. I guess I just wanted to let you know where I was and say thank you for getting my stuff from Jessop's. So, thank you.'

'No worries.' I take a swig of my beer. 'So you still want to stay at Couper's, then?' I have to say I was half-expecting that Janey'd ask to stay with me and Nina.

'Yeah, think so.'

'You don't want to stay with us until you sort everything out?'

Janey says she'd only get in the way. Then she pats Couper on the knee and says, 'Let's go then.' Couper gives her an annoyed look. Can't say I blame him. Who wants to be in such a goddamn rush when we've got a fridge full of beer?

'Come on,' says Janey.

What Janey probably doesn't realise yet is that Couper doesn't like being told what to do at the best of times, let alone being told to do something *now*. I hold back my smile and wait for his inevitable smart-arse blow off.

But it doesn't come.

Instead, Couper stops looking annoyed at Janey and starts looking apologetically at me. Says he's suddenly feeling a little tired himself. He quickly sculls his beer and stuffs Janey's in his jacket pocket.

'One for the road Mico?'

'Sure.'

I try not to act surprised. I say that I was going to bed anyway and I turn off the TV. Then I take my beer to the sink and tip the rest of it out. As soon as I hear Couper and Janey shut the front door behind them I grab a fresh cold beer and turn the TV back on and I sit there and finish off most of the beer in the fridge and then I crash on the couch for a while because I don't want to go to bed and risk waking Nina and stinking out the place just in case I've had more beers than I think.

Chapter seven
Exploding heads and epileptic jellyfish

Nina doesn't want to go to work in the morning. She's crook in the guts. Reckons she was feeling bloody awful when she got home last night. So that was it. I thought she was just tired out. She's decided to go off the pill for a while, see if that makes any difference. I point out that the pain was worse before she took the pill. I'm not trying to win any debates. It's her body. But I do point it out.

'Uh huh,' she says. 'That's interesting. Do you think then, that maybe you could pick up some condoms at some stage?'

Condoms. I hate them. Neen hates them too. She must be serious. Damn it.

'Sure. I'll get some later.'

'Thanks honey. And maybe some Nurofen as well.'

'Sure.'

'And honey, thanks for not coming in drunk and waking me up last night. You did very well, my beautiful boy.'

I smile. I always smile when she calls me her beautiful boy.

I grab the phone and call Mick the prick for her. I tell him she's been up all night with food poisoning. I say she's too crook and too asleep to talk and she won't be able to come in today. He sounds more annoyed that he's going to have to ring around and find someone else than he does concerned for Nina. He doesn't even ask how she is. I listen to him tell me about his problems with people who ring up sick at short notice and then I say 'Okay Mick, thanks Mick,' and hang up and say 'you stupid prick.' Then, without thinking, I go to Neen and try to touch her between her legs but she pushes my hand away and tries to smile and says she really does feel quite crook and she wants to go lie down for a while.

Poor bloody girl. I figure I'll piss off and let her get some rest. Maybe go hang out with Couper or something. But first I need a smoke. I'm rummaging through a pile of papers and old tobacco and shit that I keep on my side-cupboard and I come across a Centrelink appointment card. Shit. I'm supposed to be at a compulsory information seminar in less than an hour. I'd completely forgotten about it. It's a goddamn miracle I saw the card. If I'd missed this session I would have missed two in a row. The bastards start reducing your payments when you do that.

The phone rings just as I'm heading out the door. It's some home loan guy wanting to know if I've got a minute to speak. I tell him I don't and that I'm hungover as shit but he says I have a chance to win a trip to New Zealand. Obwigation fwee.

'Obligation what?'

'Obwigation fwee.'

The guy's got some sort of a speech impediment. He sounds like that goddamn Mr Magoo. I tell him I'm not interested in buying anything. He says he's not twying to sell anything. He says the whole deal is obwigation fwee. That all I have to do is come awong to a home woan seminar and wisten to the speaker. I'm not obwiged to take out a woan, nor do I even have to commit to any further business contact with the company. Just for turning up to the seminar, I go into the dwaw for a ten day twip to New Zeawand. 'It's obwigation fwee.'

Obligation free my arse. 'Okay. So, if I go to your home loan seminar, you'll give me a chance to go to New Zealand, right?'

'That's wight. Obwigation fwee.'

'So do I have to go to the seminar?'

'Well, yes, but you don't have to take out a woan.'

'But am I obliged to go to the seminar?'

'Yes, well, you have to go to the seminar to enter the dwaw.'

'Well, isn't that an obligation?'

'But, my fwiend, you are not obwiged in any way to take out any woans and you still go into the dwaw for an international howiday.'

'But that's not the point,' I say. 'The point is that it's not obligation free, because I'm obliged to go to your seminar.'

There's a pause on the other end of the line while the guy tries to get his head around what I've said. I don't wait for him to compute, the bloody time-waster. I hang up and head for the door. I'm already running late for my own goddamn seminar.

It's only after I make a bolt for the bus that I realise how hungover I am. I shouldn't have run. I shouldn't have wasted my energy like that. Some days I need energy just to stay calm. It's less than ten stops to the Centrelink office but as I plant myself in a seat I'm already starting to feel nervous. There's too much noise and I can hear it all. If it's not the bus gears grinding it's the kid crying three seats up or the wanker in tracksuit pants talking too loud on his mobile phone or someone else's phone ringing or the two girls behind me yapping about their workmates. I suddenly feel like I'm going to faint. My left hand is tingling. Is it because I'm gripping the seat rail too tightly or because I'm about to have a heart attack? Is this where I'm going to die? On a goddamn bus with some tosser bellowing into his mobile phone? I'm starting to breathe short and shallow. I loosen my grip but my hand won't stop tingling. I'm sweating like a soup vegetable. My head feels like it's about to explode. Or like it's already imploded. I can feel blood pulsing against the insides of my skull, my neck, my arms. I'm going to fuckin' spew or fall out of my seat or scream or something.

The last time this happened I was on the bus to another Centrelink seminar. I thought I was going to have a stroke or a heart attack or something even worse. I had to get off. I trembled all the way to the pub, like a walking vibrator with dying batteries. I told myself I'd be all right as soon as I got a beer to calm my nerves. But I can't get off the bus today, I can't risk the bastards cutting my payments. I'm stuck with the screaming baby and this wanker on the phone and the two girls yapping and my goddamn chest getting tighter by the breath. My brain is stuck in a panic blender. I try and tell myself it won't last. But it seems like forever.

Then suddenly I'm not thinking about dying anymore. I'm staring down at the bitumen outside the bus window, not thinking about a thing except that I feel even more exhausted. And even though time and energy are against me, I get off the bus one stop early. I need a short walk to get myself feeling normal again.

I reach the Centrelink office with a minute to spare. The guy who's giving the seminar is wearing a single dangling silver earring. His nametag says Neville. He looks a little awkward and he's a bit overweight. He's got about the same size beergut as me. Not huge, but enough to hang a fold over the shorts. I wonder whether that silver earring might be a signal that he's gay or just that he's an individual—or perhaps he just forgot to put the other one on. I wonder whether he's in a relationship or whether he has to jack off instead. Whether that earring jiggles like an epileptic jellyfish as he hunches over his bathroom sink and tries not to look in the mirror.

I wonder if he was wearing it at his own job interview. Thankfully, even though he's a fashion mistake, he's not too much of a prat. Hardly any of the Centrelink people are, these days. You do get the odd Nazi, but on the whole they seem to be aware of the reality that there are far more unemployed people than there are jobs.

I wonder whether Neville hates his job. I wonder whether he does thirty of these seminars a week and if maybe he really hates it like Nina hates working for Mick the prick, but he keeps doing them because he doesn't want to become one of the faces that are looking back at him right now. Maybe that's what keeps him in this job, the fact that he liases with the alternative day in and day out.

Or maybe he likes his job. He does seem kind of proud. He keeps using the term 'we' when he talks about Centrelink making payments. I wonder why. It's not like he is personally forking out money. There is no 'we' in the room. There is just him, doing his job, and us, a group of strangers pretending to listen. In the end, he's bowing to the same faceless authority as his audience. He's a lackey for the rule-makers we never get to see, there to remind us that they do exist and they can and will stop our payments if they see fit.

But I don't want to dump on Neville with the one earring. Like I say, he seems like a nice enough guy. He's just not telling me anything I don't already know. The last time I tuned in properly, he was saying something about how you can only claim an allowance if you have assets worth less than $149,000. Jesus Christ. Why is he wasting his breath? Right now, I don't have assets worth a hundred and forty-nine bucks. And I don't see how I'm going to have much more than that for the rest of my life, let alone while I'm on the dole. So I tune out until I hear him say we can go. Then the bunch of us file slowly out the door and everyone walks away from each other as fast as they can. It's as if each person thinks they are here because of some mistake and they don't want to associate with a bunch of dole bludgers. It shits me how being on the dole has become so shameful that even the unemployed are embarrassed to be seen with each other.

I decide to walk home instead of catching the bus. I walk a lot. I love taking different routes and discovering streets and places I've never seen before. Like the day I came across a partly demolished plasterworks in the industrial area by the train tracks that run out of town. The place was deserted because it was a Sunday so I wandered through to check it out. It was brilliant. There were statues and plaster casts everywhere. Half-wrecked rooms with danger signs hanging up. Around the back there was the wreck of a car lying among the overgrown grass. It still had its numberplates on: SVF 163. I decided to take them home and stick them up on my wall or something. I found this old pallet knife thing covered in plaster, lying in the grass. It took me ages but I managed to use it as a flathead screwdriver and get the bastards

71

off. Then I had a bit more of a look around the junk pile and I thought I saw a snake but it might have only been a lizard and then I continued on my way, two number-plates richer. I've still got 'em too. Stuck up on a wall I think, or something.

I walk in the front door and Neen gives me the phone. 'It's the dalek.'

'Hi Mum.' Before she can say anything I give her the drill. 'I spoke to Janey last night. She's fine and she's staying with Couper for a while.'

'WHAT DO YOU MEAN SHE'S FINE AND SHE'S STAYING WITH COUPER FOR A WHILE?'

What else could that statement possibly mean, I wonder. So I repeat it and then Mum goes all quiet and I've got a real hankering for a beer so I tell her I'm late for a Centrelink seminar and can I call her back and she says okay and I hang up. Ten minutes later I'm at the pub, sitting on my own. Nina's feeling a bit better and she's going to join me but she wants to have a shower first. I couldn't wait for her. It's been one of those days already, and I've only been awake for a few hours.

Chapter eight
Wardrobe head

It's more than a week before I catch up with Couper again. When I see him he looks even more serious than last time. He's been pleading his case down at the funeral parlour. His boss heard him out and then kicked him out. What's more, he wants Couper to pay for the van repairs. As if Couper can afford it. He can't even afford wheels for himself. That's why he was driving the van in the first place.

He's shaved his head. Completely. Gone right down to the bare skin on his scalp with a razor. He said he always wanted to, and now that he hasn't got a job he thought he might as well. It makes him look like a hard bastard, but also a sophisticated one—like he should be walking around with a pierced cock and a cat-o'-nine-tails at a B&D party. Maybe he should be, but he's not. Instead he's sitting on the ground with me, leaning against a wall at some sixteen-year-old kid's house. We're at a party with Janey and her friends. They're all boozing and there's a fair bit of pot floating around. The last thing I want to do is hang out with a bunch of kids. It's embarrassing. But Couper insisted we come. Reckons he's going to watch out for Janey until she gets on her feet. Doesn't want her getting into any more trouble. I'm thinking that should probably be my job except that I don't feel right about trying to do it.

Couper tells me he has to go to court in a few months. He can drive if he wants until then but now he doesn't have a car. Or a job to drive to. 'So what's the fucking point?' he says. And he has one. I notice that Couper is drinking straight bourbon. He's already gone through the best part of a bottle and it's only about eight o'clock. He must notice the slightly concerned look on my face because he sneers, 'Don't worry, I've got another one inside.'

'Yeah, whatever.'

Couper doesn't usually drink spirits. He's been known to turn into the world's biggest dickhead when he's had a few proof drinks. Tonight he's got that look in his eye like he does when he's going to let loose. But I don't care what he does. I'm not his mother. Anyway, a few drinks might help the poor guy relax.

Pretty soon I realise the party's in about as full swing as it's going to get. There's a few kids playing drinking games. A couple of guys are playing a game where they sit opposite each other and take turns trying to lob bottle-caps into each other's glass of beer. If one gets his in, the other has to scull his whole glass of beer and try not to swallow the bottlecap in the process. You usually play first to eleven. It's a simple game but a fun one and I used to be quite good at it in my school days. I mention this to Couper and we wander over to have a closer look. Couper doesn't want to play but he can see how keen I am to have a crack at these young fellas, so he says he'll watch a round or two. He's pepping up a bit. Maybe the bourbon's helping.

I settle down opposite some confident young buck who calls himself Cal and away we go. The trick to this game is to hit early and hit a few in a row. That way you get your opponent so gassed up from sculling beer that all he can think about is trying to burp without spewing. Then he can't concentrate on his own throws and you basically have free reign. Plus, the more he has to scull, the more drunk he gets and pretty soon it's goodnight nurse.

I'm on fire from the start. I don't even have a warm up. Swoosh. I nail the first one. The kid shakes his head and picks up his glass.

'Top that one up son,' I tell him, because I splashed out some of the beer with my shot. He doesn't look too happy but he complies. He downs the lot, shakes his head again, refills and then shoots about a foot wide of my glass. I sink the next one in his beer straight away. It's another splasher. 'Don't forget to top that one up as well.'

The kid nods and does it again. Then he lets out an almighty burp and tells me with a smile 'Okay buddy, you're going down.'

He's full of shit. The only thing that's going down is

more beer for him. His next throw lobs onto my right thigh. I shake my head, give him a blank stare for effect and then bang. Swoosh. It's three in a row. I remain expressionless because I want to seem intimidating, but secretly I'm pretty chuffed. Even for a marksman, this is not a bad effort. The kid doesn't wait for me to say anything. He tops up his glass and knocks it back, albeit a little more slowly than the others. They're pretty big glasses and I bet they seem a hell of a lot bigger when you have to down three in a row like that. Couper laughs. It's a loud laugh and it reeks of bourbon.

'Watch it mate,' he says to Cal. 'You're playing a veteran here.' Then he pats me on the back. 'Carry on Mico. I'm going to hang out inside for a bit.'

'Sure thing.'

I can't think of anything I'd rather be doing, so I keep playing while Couper goes inside and I completely kick the kid's arse 11–0. He spews up after 8–0 but to his credit he keeps going. I don't enjoy seeing the young fella in such a state but I figure it will be a good learning experience.

After I win so convincingly, a few of his cockier mates decide they want to take me on. I haven't been drinking much because I've been winning and these guys are fairly loaded already so it'll pretty much be a walk in the park. Plus, Couper's still off somewhere and I'm having fun, so I figure I'll stay for a while. And I do. I stay and I deal with two more guys and I'm up 4–0 on another one when some kid comes running up to me. 'Hey man,' he says. 'You'd better get inside. Your friend's going off his head.'

I was hoping it wouldn't happen. I knew it might. Couper and bourbon are never a good mix. I ask my opponent if we can call time out and he says 'Nah, fuck you. Forfeit.' The wily little bastard.

'Okay kid,' I say. 'I like your style. But I'll be back.'

I go inside. Couper's in one of the bedrooms. He's screaming and carrying on and every so often he kicks the door or thumps the dresser or something. He's saying over and over again 'Oh my god oh my god oh my god,' or 'no no no no no no,' or a mixture of 'oh my gods' and 'nos'. He's having a drunkard's version of a nervous breakdown. I've only seen him do this once before— the night after his big brother got put away and Couper himself put away a bottle of tequila.

Janey's talking through the door. 'Richard,' she's saying. 'Richard, do you want me to come in now?' I can't believe she's calling him Richard. I can't believe how out of line she is. Even Couper's own mother only calls him Richard behind his back.

'What happened?' I say. 'What's he doing?'

Janey reckons she doesn't know. She reckons one minute things were fine. Couper was pretty drunk and he was putting away the bourbons like there was no tomorrow but he was being fairly quiet. Next thing she knew, he was pacing around the room and talking to himself and then he smashed his drink on the kitchen floor and ran screaming into the bedroom. She isn't sure whether to go in or not because she's never seen him like this and she's a bit worried. I tell her I'm going in.

'I'm not sure you should. He said he's got a piece of glass and he'll cut anyone who goes in there. He's already threatened to break Robbo's nose.'

'Who? Couper? No way.' Couper's last drunken breakdown amounted to him squatting in the corner and bawling his eyes out like a child, not threatening to cut people up and break their noses. The man likes to make people laugh, not bleed.

I go inside and close the bedroom door behind me. Couper screams at me to get out. He's got a mad look in his eye. He's smashed the dresser mirror and he's holding a jagged piece of glass. From the way he's holding it and from the drops of blood on the carpet, the only person he's cut so far looks to be himself.

'Er ... Coups. Do you realise you've cut yourself, you big dick?'

'Shucking Fut up!'

There's an awkward pause. We stare at each other and make a sort of unspoken agreement. I can give him some stick later if I pretend to take him seriously for now. This is a tantrum that he needs to have. He's like a five-year-old stomping his feet in a supermarket. Well, a five-year-old holding a piece of jagged glass. He starts kind of half screaming and half moaning and kicking at a wardrobe. I can't understand what he's on about.

'What's up Coups? Is it the job?' No comprehensible reply. 'Is it the accident, Coups? Is it the car crash?' He won't answer me. Instead he just keeps moaning and kind of punching the air with the hand that's holding the glass. I probably get it wrong. It's probably because I'm a bit drunk that for a split second I think he's going to jab himself with the glass and so I reach out to try and steady his arm. Mistake. I hadn't realised how pumped he was and so putting my hand anywhere near him is like sticking it in a ceiling fan. The piece of glass swipes across my palm. Blood starts pissing out.

'Ah, jeez Couper! You cut my goddamn hand!'

Couper stops and looks up. Then he starts to cry. It's a real drunken cry. A sorry sob. 'I'm so sorry man,' he says. He drops the piece of glass. 'I'm so sorry man.'

I tell him I'm okay, even though we can both see blood gushing down my fingers onto the carpet.

'Oh fuck,' he starts moaning. 'Oh fuck, oh fuck, oh fuck.'

Then, without warning, he takes a few steps back and runs head-first into the wardrobe. As fast as he can. Run-up and slam. It's amazing that he doesn't break his neck. The wardrobe bangs against the wall. He does it again.

'Coups! Steady on.'

I can hear muffled, panicked voices on the other side of the bedroom door, but no one's coming in just yet. I look around the room. It looks distinctly like a parents' bedroom to me. Hell, I hope Couper doesn't do too much more damage. We've already got a broken dresser mirror and blood on the carpet. I take off my shirt and wrap it around my hand.

Couper's on his knees gripping the wardrobe by the sides and slamming his head into it. 'Come on Coups,' I say. 'Cut it out. We've got to clean this fuckin' mess up, man.'

He cries out between head-butts, but I can't understand him. Just as I'm about to go over and drag him back he head-butts a little too hard and his bald head crashes through the thin wood panel between the wardrobe doors. I hear a yell of pain echo from inside. And then 'Oh fuck, Mico. I'm stuck. Get me out man. Get me out.'

That's it. I wanted to laugh when I first got in here. Perhaps I should have. Perhaps things wouldn't have gone this far. Whatever the case, I'm laughing now.

'Couper, you dickhead. Look what you've done. You're stuck, man.'

'I'm stuck,' comes back the echo. 'Ah, fuck.' And then I hear the echo of Couper laughing too. 'I'm stuck,' he laughs. 'I'm fucking stuck.' It's a laugh of release. Mixed with a bit of crying, but it's a laugh all right.

I have to say, funny though it is, it must hurt. Apart from the initial impact of his head breaking wood, he's got it stuck in the smallest hole possible. He can't pull it back out because his ears are in the way and he'd scratch the bejesus out of his scalp as well. His neck's on a seriously awkward angle and must be pinching terribly. I go over to the wardrobe and open one of the doors and

I stick my own head in. I can see that at least Couper's smiling. I smile back. 'Want out?'

'Yes please, mate.'

'It might hurt a bit.'

'I don't care man. Just, please, get me out. I've had enough of this shit.'

I tell him to push downwards on his neck as hard as he can without tearing his throat open. I take a few steps back. Then I take a short run-up, and bang! I lift my right leg above Couper's neck and kick that middle panel as hard as I can. There's an almighty yell from Couper and then suddenly he's standing in front of me with blood streaming down his face, dripping from his chin to the floor. If the carpet wasn't totally ruined before, it sure is now.

Couper's smiling like a goddamn madman. 'Thanks man,' he says. 'You saved me, man.' I look at the wardrobe. It's a write-off. I look back at Couper. He doesn't look hard and sophisticated any more. He doesn't look like he should be walking around with a pierced cock and a cat-o'-nine-tails at a B&D party. He looks like what he is—a very drunk, jobless twenty-eight-year-old man at a teenage booze-up. But at least he's smiling.

There's a knock on the door. It's Janey telling us the cops have arrived. We go out to the front of the house to see there's also an ambulance. Janey tells me she called it when she heard me say I'd been cut. I know it's just a normal thing to do but I feel quite touched. It takes me and Couper about twenty minutes to convince the cops that we weren't having a fight. It's pretty hard work, seeing as we're both drunk and bleeding profusely. The ambos patch us up properly. Then both the cops and the ambos head off with a stern warning: 'For God's sake behave yourselves, you're too old to be carrying on like this.' Janey takes Couper home in a cab. I wanted to have a beer and talk about what just happened but Janey insisted they go and Couper didn't seem to mind. So I go back inside and find that cheeky little bastard who made me forfeit at 4–0. Then I kick his arse properly. I hit the first nine in a row and he throws up all over his own shirt.

Chapter nine
A couple of whimpering rats

My head throbs in time with the ringing phone. Christ, it must be early. And it's not only my head that's hurting. I look down at my right hand. The bandage I've been wearing for a few days now is filthy, and starting to smell. With my good hand I lean over and grab the phone and jam the receiver to my ear. 'Yep?'

It's Couper. He wants to meet in town by the Torrens. Says he's got something important to talk about. It doesn't sound like bad news. He's chirpy as all get out. Not a worry in the world.

'How's the head?'

He laughs. 'Never better mate. Knocked some fuckin' sense back into me. Know what I mean? How soon can you make it?'

'Give me a couple of hours. Oh yeah, and the hand's fine, thanks for asking.'

On my way I stop at a café near the Festival Theatre for a quick bite. From the service counter I can see a fat woman lying on her side in the courtyard, whimpering. She sounds a bit like a scared rat. There are a couple of ambos with her and one of them is strapping an oxygen mask over her face. I order a cheese and tomato sandwich and a small bottle of coke. Then I go and sit down and watch what's going on.

A few minutes later the waiter brings me my cheese and tomato sandwich and my small bottle of coke and sees me staring and tells me the fat woman just had some kind of a fit. I look at her spread out on the bitumen among the snapped plastic spoons and scrunched-up serviettes. She's an extremely large lady with an unkempt shock of red hair. Her eyes look as if they are about to pop out of their sockets. She doesn't seem completely sane but I'm not sure whether that's because she's just had a fit or because she's actually mentally impaired.

The ambo guy is talking to her in a cheery sing-song voice and telling her to stay calm and that everything will be all right. He's stroking her head and she seems to appreciate it. I don't know how he does it. Her whimpering would drive me crazy. The female ambo comes over with some sort of plastic plank. She lies it down next to the woman and gently tells her they're going to have to roll her onto that so that they can lift her up to the proper stretcher. The fat woman immediately starts to panic but the ambos are already working as they're talking and they manage to roll her over without too much of a scene.

Then I start wondering just how the hell they're going to lift her. I mean, this lady is big. They might need a hand. There's a couple of elderly women standing around looking concerned and a younger guy who looks like he's about to throw a wobbly himself. Neither looks like they would be much help lifting. The ambo is gently explaining to the fat lady that she should try not to wriggle because they don't want her to fall off the plank. I'm munching on my cheese and tomato sandwich and starting to think maybe I should offer to help. Just as I'm toying with the idea, the ambos count to three and hoist her up. It's not easy. They nearly lose her. The fat lady panics and wriggles and for the first time the male ambo doesn't use his cheery sing-song voice. 'Don't move,' he gasps. His face is reddening. I can see a vein in his right temple bulging. Up front, the female ambo's legs are beginning to buckle. The fat woman's still wriggling and I start thinking she's going to fall but then one of the elderly women comes over and steadies her just long enough for the ambos to plonk the plank onto the stretcher.

The whole shift only took about fifteen seconds but both of the ambos have raised a sweat. The man puts his hand against the small of his back and the vein in his temple begins to subside. The ambo woman is pretty stocky but she looks beat as well. Their patient is freaking out even more now after the shock of being lifted like that. She's whimpering big time and breathing way too rapidly. Now she really does sound like a scared rat. She sounds like that first rat I killed when I lived in Rosewater. The one that lay in a pool of its own blood, petrified and dying on my kitchen floor.

It was a real shithole, my flat in Rosewater. The landlord cared about the place so little that he let me write on the walls. I didn't have hot water the whole time I lived there so I hardly showered. I used to go to bed sticky and smelly with the day's sweat. One night I was lying there sticky and smelly in bed and I felt something run across the mattress. Something big enough to give me a feeling of pure dread. I turned on my bedside light and grabbed the baseball bat that I kept handy. I could see the curtains moving slightly so I gave them a poke and suddenly, out bolted a huge dirty rat. It rushed straight across the floor, through my bedroom doorway and down the hall. I sat there for a minute and waited for my heart to stop racing. Then, before I went back to sleep, I cleaned away all the empty beer bottles and pizza cartons from my bedroom floor.

The next day I bought a rat trap. It was like a mouse-trap, only bigger. And if it snapped down on your hand it would probably break every finger. I put a big hunk of cheese in that trap and set it right next to the stove. That night I was woken by a massive bang and the most disturbing panicked squeals I have ever heard. It was like the sound of someone or something being tortured. In my half-asleep state I'd sort of forgotten about the rat trap. I mean, I knew it was there, but I kind of didn't as well. I grabbed my baseball bat and walked quickly to the kitchen. When I flicked on the light I felt sick. The trap hadn't managed to break the rat's neck. It must have tried to get away and the trap had just caught the top half of its head. The poor thing was still very much alive and in great shock. The trap and the rat had fallen off the bench to the kitchen floor and the rat was half-pushing and half-dragging the trap around the floor as it struggled frantically to get free. And it was leaving a great trail of blood as it went. I could see its brains half hanging out. I stood there stunned and sickened, thinking *I did this. I can't believe I did this.* And all the time, that goddamn incessant squealing.

I don't know how long it was before I acted. Probably less than a minute. I stepped over to the rat, keeping my bare feet well clear of the blood smears on the floor. I could have sworn the little bastard was looking me right in the goddamn eye as I positioned my baseball bat above its head. I still wonder what it was thinking when I dashed its brains out over my kitchen floor. It was the ugliest thing I'd ever done but at least it stopped the squealing. When I was satisfied the rat was dead, I removed it from the trap and wrapped it up in newspaper. I felt so guilty. And I felt stupid for feeling guilty. After all, I eat meat. I'm indirectly responsible for the cruel deaths of animals all the time. But it was very different doing the actual killing myself—especially when I wasn't even killing something to eat it, but purely because it had wandered into my territory. I felt terrible. I took the rat outside and buried it. Then I looked up to the sky and said a quick prayer for it. Like I said, you've got to respect the dead. And I took it very seriously, the death of a rat. Then I went back to bed.

The next night I set the trap again, just to prove to myself that the house was rat free.

But it wasn't. Two a.m. and pop went the fucking weasel. This time the trap broke the rat's neck. It was a bloodless kill. It was dead by the time I got to the kitchen but I swear this one was looking at me too, as I wrapped it up in newspaper. It was a rainy night but I took it out and buried it next to its brother and said a quick prayer and then I reset the trap and went back to sleep. Not an hour passed before another snap woke me up. Another dead rat in my kitchen. I wrapped it up but it was really getting too wet outside to do the whole burial thing so I dashed out and chucked it in the wheelie bin. I said a quick prayer for it as I was running back inside. Then I reset the trap and went back to bed. I didn't catch any more rats that night, but the next afternoon when I got home there was another one slowly bleeding to death on the kitchen floor like the first. I was pretty pissed off about the mess. There was bright red blood everywhere. I grabbed the baseball bat to finish it off and then scooped it up with a dustpan and chucked it in the bin. The only prayer I said was that there be no more goddamn rats anywhere.

It was a prayer that went unanswered. I killed another nineteen of the bastards before I moved out. I must have wiped out the whole local population. I became quite good at it. Quick and methodical. It wasn't something I was proud of being good at though. Not like those ambos can be proud of what they do.

With one hand still gently squeezing his sore back, the ambo guy bends down to the woman's ear and uses his cheery sing-song voice again. 'Now that wasn't so bad was it?' Then he tells her they're going to strap her in and take her to the ambulance. The female ambo straps her in and gives her a reassuring smile. The fat woman has calmed down a bit. At least, she's stopped whimpering.

I swallow the rest of my coke and burp and go to meet Couper who I've spotted standing by the Torrens. When he sees me he gives a wicked grin. 'Mico, my good man, how are we today?'

'Fine. What's so important?'

'Uh-uh,' he holds up his hand. 'Too many people around. Come.'

We walk further along the riverbank, sit down and then don't say much at all, just stare out across the river. I get the sense Couper is working himself up to something so I don't break the silence. I sit and watch his face. He looks like he can't quite relax. He's gently crinkling a beer can in his hand and I wouldn't say his eyes are dancing but he definitely looks keyed up about something. We sit there for a good few minutes before I lose my patience. 'So what is it then?'

He reaches into his backpack and pulls out another can of beer, throws it to me. It's warm but I'll drink it anyway. Couper cracks a sly smile. 'Wanna help me rob the bastards?'

Chapter ten
This is the lounge room

He's talking about the bastards at the funeral parlour. Couper knows the security code for the alarm system because he used to drop off dead bodies after hours. He also knows the safe combination from sneaking looks over his old boss's shoulder. It's a simple plan, he reckons. We wait for the last Sunday night of the month, when the safe is going to have the most money in it, then we walk in, take the money and walk out. We'll be fine as long as there's no one hanging around doing a last-minute all-night embalming or something, and that's not likely. Couper reckons hardly anybody has their funeral on a Monday. 'I mean, what a way to start the week,' he says. He reckons that even if there was someone working back late, we'd realise before we got in too deep. 'But it's just not gonna happen. At one o'clock on a Monday morning, the only people on the premises will either be us, or dead.'

It sounds easy enough, this breaking and entering stuff. After all, it's not like there'll be an alarm going off or anything. And Couper knows the place like the back of his hand. All we really need to worry about is borrowing a car for the night.

'Big Stan's purple Kingswood,' he suggests.

'Jeez Couper, I don't know about that.' I've never asked to borrow my dad's car before. I've always assumed he wouldn't give it to me if I did.

'Well, maybe we could borrow the Kartiniski-mobile for the night?'

Pffffffffffff. I wipe down my chin and shake my head at the wastage frothing on the grass at my feet. 'That doesn't even deserve an answer.'

'Okay, okay. Forget that. But I still think we should try for Big Stan's.'

I shrug. Even if I could get the purple Kingswood, I'm not sure I'd want to use it in a goddamn robbery. I mean—who knows where they have security cameras these days? The last thing I'd want is the car being traced back to my dad. Christ, he'd never take me to a front bar again.

As if he'd read my mind, Couper points out that we can swap my dad's numberplates with those ones I found in the plasterworks. Just for the night, and then we'll return his car in the morning exactly like we found it. I can't argue with that. And asking Dad for his car is at least a realistic option compared with asking Nina for hers. She's going to be against this thing enough as it is, without aiding and abetting us. 'All right,' I say. 'I'll give it a crack.'

There's only one thing left to discuss. 'How much money are we talking about?'

Couper reckons he doesn't know for sure, but something like a few thousand dollars. It depends how much cash people have laid down over the past few weeks as funeral deposits. 'Some of those bloody tax-dodgers pay for the whole lot in cash, mate,' he says. 'It won't exactly be the heist of the century, but we should still be laughin'.'

I am laughing. 'You might even be able to pay for the van repairs.'

'Yeah, right.' Coups chuckles.

I have to tell Nina. We don't keep things from each other. Plus, I'm curious to know whether there's any chance she'll think I should go through with it. Or whether she'll just think I'm a fuckin' idiot. I tell her later that night.

'You're a fuckin' idiot,' she says. 'Whatcha want to go and do something like that for? You want to end up in jail? Bloody hell, Mico.'

I tell her not to worry. That even if we got caught we probably wouldn't end up in jail. 'I mean, it's not like armed robbery or something. And the way the courts are these days, we'd probably get off with a suspended sentence. Plus,' I say, 'think of the money.'

'Think of the hell that your dad'll give you when he finds out you've used his car to rob a fuckin' funeral home. I mean, c'mon Mico. You're stealing money that people have paid to have their bloody loved ones buried.'

'They're not all "bloody", Neen.' I try and win her over

with a cheeky smile. It doesn't work. So I put on a serious face and I tell her I'm sure the funeral parlour is insured for that sort of thing anyway. She says that still doesn't make it right. That's when I pull out the card that Couper suggested I play. 'What about you stealing from Mick the prick?' I say. 'What's the difference?'

Nina says the difference is she won't get caught. 'Anyway,' she says, 'Mick's a bloody prick and he deserves it.'

'You're a hypocrite. Stealing is stealing is stealing.' I don't actually mean that, but it sounds good.

'Yeah? Well, you're a shit.' Conversation temporarily over. She leaves the house and slams the front door so hard a bunch of dried flowers fall off the wall and the goddamn petals go everywhere.

I am a shit sometimes. I'm more than aware of it. But this time I genuinely don't feel like I'm being a shit. Aside from the fact that I do actually believe she's a hypocrite, I can't help thinking I'm doing it for us. Even though Nina never gives me a hard time, I'm sick of bludging money off her. I mean, doing housework is one thing but it'd be nice, just for a while, to be able to pay my way. Plus, if I get enough, there's even a chance she could quit working for Mick the prick and give herself some breathing space to look around for something else.

I sit down on the couch and crack a longneck of Melbourne. I've barely swallowed the first mouthful when there's a knock on the door. Neen must have forgotten her keys. So much for storming out. I decide against making a smart comment, she's liable to really get stuck into me if I do. Still, I can't help smiling as I swing open the door.

'Glad to see you're happy as Larry bloody Emdur. Meanwhile your mother's home raving at her bowl of carrot and ginger·soup and I'm climbing the walls and your sister won't speak to either of us.' It's my dad.

'Dad. Isn't it a bit late for you to be coming around?' It doesn't make much sense saying this because, quite frankly, any time is strange for my dad to be coming around. It's the first time he's been to our house.

'Never mind the time,' he says and points at my beer. 'Got one of them for me?'

'Sure.' I show him into the lounge room. We stand there staring at each other for a few seconds. His face looks flaccid, pale, lifeless. Like one of the sun-faded deflated beach balls that lie around for years in the garden around his pool.

'This is the lounge room,' I say, and head off to get his beer.

It's the best conversation opener I can come up with. I wish I could start up with some light, mutually enjoyable point of reference. But I have no point of reference with him. Nothing in common. Except, I guess, the man doesn't mind a beer. 'Wanna glass?' I yell from the kitchen.

'Yeah.'

I pour some beer from my longneck into a schooner

I stole from the pub and I take the glass into the lounge room for him and the rest of the bottle in for me and when I get there he says, 'So this is the lounge room.'

I nod. 'Yeah it's the lounge room all right.'

'Nice flowers.'

'Yeah.'

'What are they doin' all over the floor?'

I shrug and sip my beer. 'How's Mum?'

'She thinks Janey's never coming back.'

'She'll come back. She just has to feel like she's allowed to live her life the way she wants to.' It's my attempt at a compromising viewpoint and it's a mistake.

My dad's beach ball face inflates into a fat scowl. He points a finger at me and brings his voice up to a low-level yell, like a coach giving someone a dressing down. 'Not under my roof,' he warns. 'I'm not having her flashing her tits to anyone she likes while she's living under my roof.'

He's started to get all flushed. It amazes me how worked up he gets. I mean, I'm not Janey. Why is he getting mad with me? Maybe he can sense that I don't really care whether she goes home or not. But that's my business. Anyway, all I want is to sit here and not be yelled at. Even low-level yelled at. All I want is to tell him he's under my roof now so he can just bloody well chill out.

But I don't get a chance. He stands up. And now it's a high-level yell. A down-by-twenty-points-going-into-the-last-quarter yell. 'And it might be fine for you and Nina and all your bloody flowers but it's nowhere near good enough for our Janey! Do you hear me?! NOWHERE NEAR GOOD ENOUGH!'

I shrug. I don't know what his point is, but I'm sure he feels he's made one. I could probably make a few myself but there's not much use. Some people just can't get through to each other. He must start thinking the same thing because he doesn't say anything else and we sit there in silence while we finish our beers. The truth is, he's not really pissed off at me and I'm not really pissed off at him. What we're both pissed off at is the fact that, these days, the thing we are most likely to agree on is that we are in a lounge room.

When he finishes his beer he says, 'Speak to Janey will you? Try and talk some goddamn sense into her. At least get her to give us a ring.'

I nod. 'I'll try. Do you want another beer? I'm having one.'

Dad shakes his head.

As he's going out the door I blurt out, 'Hey, that was a nice crack you gave Jessop.'

Dad turns around. 'Did you give him one? When you went back in there?'

I shake my head. 'Nah. I was too busy getting Janey's stuff.' I can see he's disappointed. He walks to the car.

'Dad? Can I borrow the Kingswood next Sunday night?'
'What for?'

Funny. I didn't even think I'd get that far. 'I want to take Nina to the drive-in.'

'Why don't you use her car?'

I tell him I want to take *her*. Not have her take me. 'She drives me everywhere in her car all the time. I want to give her a break. Give her car a break too.'

'Maybe,' he says. 'Just talk to Janey and ring me later.'

I shut the door.

A big part of me wishes that I'd given Mr Jessop a kick in the guts that day. And not just so I'd have something to talk about with my dad, but because I realise that I'm goddamn angry about what he was doing with my sister. Same as I'm angry about what Aaron was doing with me.

I get a cold beer and go back to the couch.

Neen comes back at about midnight. She's not mad anymore even though it's apparent she still thinks I'm a shit. She sits on the couch and helps me finish off my longneck and then we go to bed and we sort of make up but we don't have sex because she's having a bit of pain. I don't reckon she's been any better since she's been off the pill but she says it hasn't even been two weeks yet. I suggest going to the doctor sometime this week. Nina says could we please not talk about doctors. So we don't talk about doctors and I lie next to her and gently kiss the back of her head while she tries to get to sleep.

Chapter eleven
Hungry German Shepherd

I'm waiting for Bob the butcher to get me some marinated lamp chops from his freezer when I see an ad stuck up in the shop window. Jessop's got a vacancy at his dental clinic, he's looking to take someone on in a junior female position. Yeah right. No fuckin' prize for guessing what position *that* is. The guy's got a bloody nerve. But he won't get any applicants—not from around here anyway. Everyone knows that something dodgy went on between him and Janey. And what they don't know for certain they waste no time making up. It's strange how these things work. Janey plays tennis in a G-string and suddenly she's the local bike. I fucked anything that moved for years and nobody knew the difference. I wonder what people would say if they knew about those first few years after Aaron. The years when I started questioning just who the fuck I was after losing my straight virginity one week and a good deal of my gay virginity the week after. The years I spent looking for answers in other people's underpants.

I was screwing women this way and that and remembering close to nothing the next day. Not that any of the sex was worth remembering. As for the guys, they were always at least forty years old. One was over sixty. Usually the sex amounted to me giving a slobbery drunken blow job. Sometimes I'd lie back and let the man play with me but more often than not I was only interested in where the next scotch was coming from and whether I could smoke in the bedroom. My drunken pick-ups invariably ended with me and my older man lying on the bed discussing whether or not we thought I was gay, or talking about what they did for a living. I met some pretty nice guys in those years. No one ever went home with me more than once though. Once they got to know me, they knew that I was on my own trip and they didn't want to mess me up. They just wanted to be friends.

I wrote to Aaron after those years and said that if he wanted to have his cock sucked by someone younger, he should have gone out to a club and met someone who knew what they were in for. Like the guys who took me home. The guys who took me home and let me smoke in their bedrooms and drink their whisky and suck their dicks if I wanted to and didn't make me if I didn't. They weren't friends of the family with sneaky plans. They were just good guys. Good gay guys. Without who, I would have probably ended up resenting gay men, instead of simply realising I wasn't one.

I remember the night I realised I wasn't gay. It was

the night of the wiry cock in the moonlight. I was plastered and I'd gone out clubbing again to try and pick up an older man. I wasn't having much luck. Maybe because I was so drunk that I couldn't walk in a straight line. Anyway, I was getting tired of waiting for someone to approach me so when I spotted this bearded bloke standing on his own, I went up behind him and I breathed into his ear: 'Want me to suck your cock?' He didn't respond. He didn't even look at me. The prick didn't even *look* at me.

'Hey, buddy.' I drunkenly poked him in the shoulder. 'You fuckin' rude prick.'

He turned around, looking surprised. Then he pointed to his ears and said like a deaf person that he was deaf. You know, just kind of mouthed the words and moaned 'I dair.'

I nearly apologised for calling him a rude prick but then I realised he wouldn't have heard me anyway so I signalled I understood and then mimed sucking a cock. He looked taken aback but let me take his hand and lead him outside. We went to a park next to a nearby train station. I sat leaning against a tree and started wetting my lips when suddenly the bearded fellow was upon me. He pulled down my jeans and started licking my dick like a goddamn hungry German Shepherd. He went on eagerly for about five minutes. I felt guilty letting him because I already knew that I wasn't going to come. I couldn't even get an erection. I sat there against the tree and I felt this man's facial hair rubbing between my thighs. I shut my eyes and I tried to enjoy it more, but

I couldn't help thinking that the whole situation was starting to feel really stupid. Almost funny. I almost laughed at where I'd ended up. And then I suddenly thought: what the hell am I doing? So I gently pushed his head away.

'Stop now,' I told him, though I knew he couldn't hear me.

He stopped and looked up and grinned and then he stood up above me and undid his pants. 'Saaaa my corrr,' he said.

'Hang on.' I started doing up my pants.

'Saaaa my corrr,' he said again and dropped his trousers. Then he took down his underpants and I could see him stretching his thin wiry dick out in the moonlight. Playing with himself. Trying to make himself hard.

'Saaaa my corrr, pleeee,' he said.

I looked at him pleading with his hungry German Shepherd eyes. I looked at his wiry white cock stretched out in the moonlight. I thought about sucking it for him, but I couldn't. I didn't want to. I got up and left the poor guy standing there between the trees and the train tracks with his pants around his ankles.

I didn't drink any more that night, not even when I got home. I sat on my couch for a few hours, thinking it all over. Thinking about what I'd been repeating for nearly seven years since Aaron first used me to play out his fantasies. I didn't have another one night stand for six months. The next person I took to bed was the same one who wakes up in it these days. The same one who's at work right now, probably wondering if I'll remember to buy marinated lamb chops.

I take down Mr Jessop's ad and stuff it in my pocket. It's not right that a guy like him is trying to hire young girls. I mean, sure, he didn't touch Janey or anything. And she wasn't pissed out of her brain either. If you ask her, she knew exactly what she was doing, but that doesn't make it right. Since when does a sixteen-year-old kid know what they're doing?

When I get home there's a message from Dad on the answering machine. I haven't rung Janey for him yet, so I decide I may as well. I pick up the phone and dial, and I get the answering machine. She's probably screening calls.

'It's me. Mico,' I say and Janey picks up. She's doesn't seem overly pleased to hear from me but at least she didn't pretend she wasn't home.

'Mico. Hi. What do you want?'

I ask how long she's planning to stay at Couper's house and tell her she's probably going to have to start paying rent soon.

'Oh, sorry, I didn't realise you were Couper's landlord,' she drones.

'Look, I think it's something you should think about. Couper's not made of money, y'know.'

'Mico, I've already given him some, okay?'

'Good,' I say, a little weakly.

'Anything else? I'm kind of in the middle of something.'

I ask her if she's spoken to Mum or Dad yet. She says

she hasn't and doesn't want to. I tell her that I really need to borrow Dad's car on Sunday night and I'll stand a far better chance of getting it if she gives him a ring, so even if she doesn't want to, can she please do it for my sake?

'Sorry Mico. Dad's an arsehole.'

'Okay. Sure, but can you think about it?'

'Maybe. See ya.'

'See ya. And just think about it, okay?'

I hang up knowing she won't. I grab a beer and sit down to figure out how I can wangle the purple Kingswood on Sunday night. Maybe I can offer to clean Mum and Dad's pool for a month. I sure know what I'm doing there and I also know they hate doing it themselves. It would mean going around once a week. That's four times. I can handle that if it means getting the car. I'll have a couple more beers and then I'll ring Dad.

I kick back on the couch and turn on the telly. There's a one-day cricket match on but they're having an ad break. Bob Sanders, the drunken talent show host, is doing a promo for his show about dog shows. Shit. That was quick. He's not going to be going it alone either. His co-host is Annelise de Jour. She's twenty-something, blonde and pretty. Typical channel nine window-dressing. She's squatting down next to a sausage dog saying how much she likes sausages. And you just know that all around the country there's thousands of losers kicking back on their couches saying, I bet you do, baby. No doubt about it. The stupid show's going to be a hit.

So I knock back a few beers in front of the cricket. It's not a great game, but good enough for me to forget about ringing Dad until the innings break. And then the phone rings just as I'm looking for it. It's Dad. Before he has a chance to say anything, I tell him it's really important that I borrow the Kingswood on Sunday night and that I'm willing to do almost anything in return. 'A month's pool-cleaning for starters,' I tell him.

'Good chocca,' he says. Whenever my dad likes something he says 'good chocca'. Don't ask me what it means, I don't have a goddamn clue. Then he says he was going to lend me the car anyway but yeah, he'd appreciate the pool cleaning. He thanks me for ringing Janey and he says she's rung them and he thinks everything's going to be all right, now that they've had a chance to talk. I can't believe she actually rang them. I must have gotten through to her after all. Great. That means I still count on some level.

'No problem Dad,' I say, coolly.

'Good chocca son.'

'So did Janey say anything about coming home?'

He tells me she said she's pretty right for now, but they didn't ask too many questions. Didn't want to push their luck.

'Yeah. Right then,' I say.

'Good chocca,' he says again. Christ. Three good choccas in one day is something of a record. I start thinking he might be about to invite me to a bar so he can ignore me again but he doesn't go quite that far. He just says I can pick up the keys to the Kingswood on Sunday afternoon and he hopes we have a good time at the drive-in. I hang up feeling pretty good. For a start, I've got the car. I've also been praised by my parents for the second time in a month. And to top it off, my little sister actually heeded my advice. I finish my beer, grab a fresh one and settle down to prepare for another Glenn McGrath onslaught. I'm looking forward to the next few hours. Nina'll be back soon and we've got cricket on the telly, marinated chops and six big bottles of beer left in the fridge. The makings of a great night.

I decide to ring Couper and tell him the good news about the car. He doesn't screen, just picks up the phone. I tell him Big Stan's purple Kingswood is all go.

'I thought it would be,' he says. 'I spoke to Janey. Told her we needed the car on Sunday so she phoned up your folks to let 'em know she was all right.'

'Oh. Great.'

'Yeah,' says Couper. 'Hey, can we maybe speak tomorrow instead? I'm pretty busy right now.'

'No problem.'

I hang up and have a slug of beer. So what do I care if Janey listens to Couper when she doesn't listen to me? McGrath will be steaming in from the Randwick End any minute. Nina's due home in an hour. There's still chops and beer in the fridge. Still all the makings of a great goddamn night.

Chapter twelve
Nosy tortoise territory

I pick up the purple Kingswood at seven o'clock on Sunday night. Dad asks where Nina is. I tell him she's at home putting on her make-up or something but the truth is she's at home in a wicked mood because she's seriously pissed off at me.

'I didn't think Nina wore make-up.'

I didn't think he ever would have noticed.

'Well she is tonight,' I lie. And I manage a grin. 'I think she's looking around for some lipstick to match the duco. It's not every night a girl gets taken out in a fine purple automobile like this one.' Not even tonight, as a matter of fact.

Dad smiles and gives me both thumbs up as I pull away. It's hard to smile back at him. Apart from the fact that I'm nervous, I'm a little uncomfortable with how mad Nina is. I hate defying her on this one.

Couper's standing out the front of his place wearing all black when I arrive. He's got black dye smeared under his eyes. He's even wearing gloves and a beanie and holding a torch and a goddamn sack. Christ, he may as well be wearing a black-and-white striped shirt and a robber mask. Carrying a big sign saying 'PROFESSIONAL FUCKIN' THIEF'.

'Jeez Couper, where's your balaclava?'

Couper reaches up and pulls his beanie down over his face. He's cut out eye holes and a mouth hole.

'For fuck's sake Coups! Take it off.'

'You asked,' he grins, as he rolls it back atop his head.

We're lucky Couper has no neighbours like Mrs Beveringham. They probably would have called the cops on us already.

'Have you got the drill?'

Couper says it's in his sack.

When we get back to my house, Nina's gone. She hasn't left a note. I don't think she'd actually leave me over this, but I check the garage just to be sure. Her car's still there. I relax a bit—she's probably gone for a walk to let off some steam. Couper and I get a couple of beers and we take the Kingswood out to the back lane to swap the numberplates. There's a slight hitch. Couper left his sack with the drill in it on his driveway.

'No worries, I'll go get it,' he says. 'Can I take the Kingswood?'

'Go ahead. Take the Kingswood. Just don't go crashing the fuckin' thing.'

'No worries.'

He screeches the tyres as he takes off. Idiot. I go back

inside and turn on the telly and sit on the couch and hold my beer and stare at the dried flower garden and wait for someone to come back. The clock's ticking at a snail's pace. The telly's flickering like a dying fire. I sip my beer in slow motion and wait.

The sudden ring of the phone is like the clicking fingers of a hypnotist. I rush to answer it, thinking it might be Neen. But it's not. It's that goddamn home loan seminar guy again—the exact same guy who called me last time. I can tell it's him because of his bloody speech impediment. I can't believe he's got the nerve to bother me on a Sunday. He goes straight into a sales pitch. He's going on about how beautiful New Zeawand is. How it's the home of 'Wawd of the Wings'.

'Are there any hobbits there?'

He laughs that fake salesman laugh and tells me 'good one, sir'.

'Good one yourself. Now, tell me. Are there any hobbits there?'

There's a hint of a nervous chuckle and then a pause. I think he's trying to get his bearings, work out whether he heard me correctly. Then, having decided that he probably did, he ignores my verbal spanner and pushes on with the works.

'Now ... um ... sir, if you would wike come to one of our obwigation fwee seminars, we can discuss your home woan further. And you can also enter our dwaw to win an obwigation fwee trip to New Zeawand.' He chuckles. 'And who knows—you might even see a hobbit. Now, if you'll just give me your details, I'll send you an invitation.'

'But mate, I'm not interested.'

'Sir,' he says, 'it's obwigation fwee.'

'Didn't you call me a couple of weeks ago?'

'Absowootwee not sir. That's impossible. This is oanwee my second shift.'

'I don't believe you,' I say. 'I'm on to you Magoo. Now PISS OFF. D'ya hear me?'

I don't hang up the phone. I just sit back on the couch and lean my ear against the receiver. The home loans guy isn't saying anything either and it takes him about fifteen seconds to hang up. I put the receiver down and shut my eyes and try to will Nina home.

The slamming of the front door wakes me up. I look at the clock. It's nearly midnight. I hear whistling and the sound of boots approaching. Goddamn Couper. He said he'd be quick. He's been gone almost four hours. So much for sitting down and going through the plan with a fine-tooth comb.

He stomps up the corridor. 'Sorry I took so long. Had some shit to do.'

I'm too half-asleep to be properly annoyed. We take the car back out to the lane and swap the plates over and then rush through the final preparations for the robbery. Couper takes me through the basic plan. It's not too complicated. Still, I'm starting to get a bit nervous. And

I'm worried about where Neen's got to. I'm even starting to think I should maybe stay home and let Couper do it all himself. I can't say anything though. It's too late now. When the clock ticks over to one a.m., we leave.

As we pull up across the road from the funeral parlour Couper rolls down his balaclava again. I'm still not sure about this balaclava thing. I think he looks more stupid than anything else. We sneak around the back. Attached to the rear of the main building there's a maintenance shed. It's locked with a bolt, like the ones you get on a big pair of driveway gates. The bolt drops into a cylindrical hole in the cement floor. You can't unlock it from the outside unless you've already attached a piece of wire on the inside and pulled it through the gap in the door. Somebody has.

'Couper,' I whisper. 'I thought you only decided to do this after you got fired.'

He shrugs. 'I did. Kind of.'

The parlour's fitted out with a basic motion alarm. It'll pick up any movement higher than two feet off the ground. Because we are entering from the back shed, we'll have to crawl on our stomachs army-style until we get close enough to the alarm console to disable it. We should be all right. It's a pretty archaic system. Couper says there's an outside chance it's not even turned on. The family who run this business are pretty slack about security. Still, once we're inside the shed, we play it safe and stay on our bellies.

When I feel my partly exposed stomach shift from cool concrete to scratchy red carpet, I start realising we're actually doing this. We're one step away from not being able to turn back. I can see the faint pink glow of the alarm system console out of the corner of my eye. It's alive, I reckon. I whisper this to Couper and he agrees. It's time to be real careful now. It seems like we're crawling along for ages. Then the sole of Couper's shoe on my forehead tells me to stop. We lie there breathing for a while in the darkness and the silence for a bit and then suddenly Couper stands up. I knew he'd have to stand up eventually, but it feels bloody strange when he actually does. Makes me feel sort of alone. I'm a bit relieved when I hear his voice whisper for me to stay put. The console gives a long quiet beep. He's been detected and he'll have to punch in the right code within a few seconds or all hell will break loose. I lie there and listen to Couper press in the code. Six beeps. The console responds with a long beep of its own.

'Shit,' whispers Couper.

'What is it?'

No response. Just six quicker beeps almost immediately followed by another long one. Then a pause. Then six more beeps and again the long one. Then I hear him giggle.

'Oh fuck.'

'What is it? What's wrong?'

'They've changed the code on me. Oh fuck, I knew they would.'

I say if he knew they'd change the code then what the hell are we doing here in the first place? But neither of us can hear my voice after the first few words because our few seconds are up. And so is my heart rate. Way up. I feel like I've been jabbed through the chest with an adrenalin needle and I suddenly realise how much louder a burglar alarm sounds when it's ringing for you. I panic and shout to Couper that we should bolt. Couper switches the torch on and shines it into his own face. Then he winks and gives one of his evil cackles and ducks around behind the office counter to the safe. I block my ears to try and stop myself freaking out. I'm frozen to the spot, wishing I wasn't a robber. Thinking every shadow is a cop coming out of the darkness. Thinking I'm about to bump into Constable Ben McPhenton again. I can see it now: 'So what're you doing these days Millevic?' he'd say, as he bundled me into the back of a paddywagon. 'Actually, Ben, I'm just robbing the dead at the moment,' I'd tell him, even though I'd know he wouldn't be listening because he really couldn't give a fuck.

To Couper's credit, he's pretty quick. He finds the safe key, spins the right combination—thank God they didn't change *that*—and comes bounding back with three or four calico bags.

'This is it I reckon. More than I thought. Let's get the fuck out of here.'

We're inside the car in a matter of seconds. I pull away as fast as I can without squealing the wheels and I shit you not, we make it about twenty metres down the road before the car conks out. I look at the petrol gauge. Empty. I can't believe it.

'Oh shit,' says Couper. 'I forgot to fill her back up.'

I sit there stunned. I can't believe he's used all the petrol. I have another go at starting it and when it's clear we're not going anywhere, we get out and push the Kingswood to the side of the road. That goddamn alarm is still going bananas. We have to leg it, and quick. The only thing is, we don't want to leave the bags in the car just in case the cops decide to search it. Nor do we want to be running around the streets at three in the morning with a bunch of money bags in the immediate vicinity of a robbery. We need to lay low somewhere nearby. There's a schoolyard across the road.

'Shit, Coups. The bloody neighbours will be out in a minute.'

'Bullshit. No one cares about alarms these days.'

He's probably right. Still, we need some cover. The cops aren't here yet but they will be any second. So the schoolyard it is. It's a big risk but we don't have much other choice. We sprint over and climb up inside a piece of play equipment that looks like one of those shitty plastic spacey things you see outside fast food restaurants. We can see the funeral parlour across the road through a gap in the plastic. From that distance it would be impossible to see us in here, especially at night. A cop would have to come right over and climb up the slippery dip.

We sit there not moving, nervous as hell, even though somehow Couper is still grinning. The alarm cuts out about twenty minutes later. Then someone comes out the front and starts poking around the parlour premises with a torch. We're too far away to hear him properly, but from the way he's slashing that torchlight around, we can tell he's pretty pissed off.

'I think it's John Burroughs,' Couper whispers. 'My old boss.'

'Shhh,' I say and we both sit tight. Ten minutes later, Couper's old boss is still out there. Every now and then he flashes the torchlight in our direction and I get the sickening feeling that he's weighing up whether to come and check out the playground or not. My dread is interrupted.

'Mico. I need to do a shit.'

'You fuckin' what?'

'I'll jump down on the woodchips.'

'No way. No bloody way Couper. That guy keeps flashing his light over here as it is. If he spots you we're goners. Anyway, how can you think about doing a shit right now?'

'I can't help it mate, it's the fuckin' excitement. The adrenalin. It's sent my guts into a frenzy. I gotta go Mico. I really gotta.'

'Oh, for Christ's sake.'

But the thing is, as soon as I see him drop his pants and squat I get an ominous gut rumble of my own. I can't explain it. It's like I've become a bottle of champagne that someone's been shaking for a minute or two and now I need to take the cork out or I'm going to explode.

'All right then. I'm taking the other corner,' I say.

'Hoo hoo,' Couper chuckles to himself. And he lets one go.

'Oh for God's sake. Try not to fart, will you? I'm trying to pretend that this isn't happening.'

Talk about waving a red flag at a bullfrog. He's starting to drown out the goddamn crickets. And squatting in the corner of some playground equipment with a turd hanging out of my behind at two in the morning, listening to Couper's incessant trumpeting and poorly restrained laughter, I find myself unable to remain serious. I start chuckling quietly and the more I chuckle, the more bowel movements I have and the more movements I have, the more I chuckle. And I start letting a few go myself.

'Hoo hoo,' laughs Couper again.

Suddenly, I can see bloody Burroughs heading across the road swinging his torch beam. He's coming our way. And I'm starting to realise what they mean by being caught with your pants down.

'Coups! Shhh! He's coming over.'

I don't know whether Burroughs has heard us or not. He's not walking with any particular urgency, but he's getting uncomfortably close.

'Oh shit Couper, I think we're going to have to leg it.'

'No fucking way. I'm only half done man. I'm still in nosy tortoise territory.'

So am I. And I'm thinking the only thing worse than riding in the back of a paddywagon right now would be riding in the back of a paddywagon with my underpants full of poo. So pulling up the duds and legging it isn't really an option. I squat there, frozen. Then I hear a car pull up and doors slam. It's the cops. Burroughs turns around and goes back over to their car. I thank God under my breath as they all go back inside the funeral parlour. As soon as we're sure they're inside, I finish up, do up my pants and use the toe of my boot to push my crap down to the woodchips below.

I lift my t-shirt over my nose and settle back down to keep watch. I should have known it'd be a while before the cops turned up. They probably had enough to worry about without rushing to help the already dead. I start wishing that I'd just walked up the road to the local service station and filled up a jerry can. I could have had Dad's car back in my driveway with the right numberplates on it by now.

They all come back outside. Burroughs says something angrily, I can't quite hear what, and then strides off around the back. I hear him rev his car and drive away. The two cops take a quick walk around and check out the cars parked nearby. They flash a torch over my dad's car, but only for a second, then they hang around the front of the parlour for maybe five minutes longer before they piss off. Me and Couper stay put. Once they're gone we relax a bit but there's no way we're going anywhere just yet.

Now and then Couper teases me by flicking the torchlight on and off quickly. That is until I wrest it off him and unscrew the top and chuck it down on the woodchips under the slippery dip. 'I hope it lands in my crap,' I tell him.

A few hours later, at first light, Couper stuffs the calico bag up his top and hides behind the front seats in the Kingswood while I walk up the road to get a jerry can. I don't have any money on me except for a bundle of fifties that Couper gave me from one of the bags. I peel one off and stick the rest into my front jeans pocket and smile. It's the first time I feel like we actually might get away with this thing. And as I'm walking up to the service station I start to wonder just how much money we got in the end.

We don't count it until we're safely back inside the house. It's far more than we thought. It's almost scary. There's over twenty-seven thousand dollars in all. Couper says there's no way they should have had that much money in the safe. Not ever. It must be a one-off. He can't believe it. He's stoked. He's cracking up laughing. I'd like to be stoked. It's just that Neen's nowhere to be seen and I'm wondering where she is. She hasn't stayed out all night since we've been together. And I have to say, at the moment, all I am is worried.

Chapter thirteen
A death worse than fate

Fact: Not all of us are going to do spectacular things with our lives. Only a relative minority ever do. The rest of us die slow, trivial, relatively meaningless deaths right from the moment we're born. The older I get, the more I feel part of this majority. I call it dying a death worse than fate.

The way I see it, there's only so many fates to go around. There's a few good ones and a few bad ones and you either get dealt one or you don't. Some people end up as rock stars, successful crayfishermen or teachers who are remembered by their students for decades. Other people end up drowning in their own soup, being trampled by runaway bull elephants or murdered by serial killers. The rest of us remain eternally unnoticed, like extras in a movie, until we waste away. Sure, I'd rather remain unnoticed than have my skull crushed by a rampaging pachyderm, but that's not the point. The point is that I don't think I have a choice.

Even now I feel like a movie extra, walking along the

hospital corridors, being bumped out of the way by busy doctors and dedicated nurses. Steamrolled by people with a purpose. And it's not just the doctors and nurses who remind me of my own insignificance. It's the goddamn lives and deaths playing out all around me. I sneak peeks as I pass wards. I see the sick and the maimed wrapped up in their starched white cocoons and I wonder why they are there. Car accidents, maybe. Emphysema. Infections. Broken eggs in the human progress omelette. Fateless. I wonder if that's what I'll become. I wonder if being fateless is a destiny in itself. At any rate, I have to put any sniff of a destiny on hold while I deal with the hospital-grade detergent stench of life's current reality.

I'm at the hospital to visit Nina. She was admitted last night because her stomach pain got so bad she could barely stand up. It's terrible news, but at least she's not dying or anything. No more than the next person, anyway. She told the doctor they're just stress pains. It makes sense, sort of. She's stressed out of her brain working for Mick the prick. The doc gave her some pethidine and kept her in overnight. This morning he wrote her a referral to a gynaecologist. She told him no thanks very much but she put the referral in her bag. I'm going to try and make her go. Not that anyone can make Nina Kartiniski do anything.

Anyway, that's why she wasn't home. Not because she was mad. She's not mad now even though I should have been there when she collapsed on the toilet floor, instead of out robbing people. Even though she had to

119

call her mother, of all people, to get a ride to the hospital. That must have hurt nearly as much as the stomach pain. Nina doesn't get along with her mother at all.

Her mother's a bitter old alcoholic at the best of times and a hard-core God-fearing bitch at the worst. She's been kicked when she's down so many times that she doesn't even bother getting up anymore. Doesn't even bother opening her eyes to see who's doing the kicking. Just lies on her back and spits foul venom bile at the world. Even spits it at her daughter. Six months ago she was plastered at a family party and she cornered Nina and asked 'when're you gonna stop sluttin' around and get fuckin' married?' Nina answered that she wasn't slutting around but that she's not sure she believes in the idea of marriage. What she got for saying that was a prompt, hard, slap across the face and a more aggressive repeat of the question.

Nina's aunt managed to come and drag Bette away before she had another crack. It was too late though. Nina was already flushed from the slap and flushed from trying not to cry. The next day I had a go at Bette, but she said she couldn't remember anything and refused to apologise. I could see it was bothering her though, because she started drinking earlier than usual. Sad thing is, her spitting venom at the world kills her even more because in her core she still knows she's a good person. She's just too goddamned scared and bitter to do anything about it. Still, she's not so far gone that she won't drive over drunk and pick up her daughter who can't drag herself off the floor for the pain. She'll complain about doing it, but she'll still do it.

So Neen's lying in a hospital bed when I tell her we're about fourteen grand better off. She's not impressed. She still thinks I'm stupid and that I shouldn't have gone against her wishes. But it's a level of unimpression that's tempered with the understanding that, thanks to my stupidity, she can now take a break from working for Mick the prick. So while she doesn't exactly congratulate me or jump for joy, she doesn't tell me to get out either. I try to explain to her why I think I had to do the robbery. I tell her about the death worse than fate stuff. I tell her I'm scared of dying alone on the couch at two in the morning, halfway through another bottle of beer and another episode of Letterman. That I actually want to do something with my life. She tells me that instead of going out and robbing funeral parlours I should cut down on my drinking.

She's sort of right, I guess. Maybe I should cut down a bit. And maybe I will. But I reckon there's something else I have to work out first. I have to work out how to get back on that goddamn bus that so many people seem to be on. The one that drives us through life along the road towards some sort of happiness. I used to be on it too, but I got off, can't remember when. And I've been sitting at the side of the road for what seems like forever, waiting for that bus to come around again. I'm desperate to get back on. I don't even care if it's a rough ride. I don't even need to *be* happy. I just need to feel like I'm going in the right direction. Going somewhere. And when I know I'm going somewhere, then I'll worry about how much beer I drink along the way.

Me and Neen sit pretty much in silence in the cab on the way home from the hospital. We hold hands and don't say much. I'm thinking about how I'm going to convince her to see the gynaecologist. As for what the problem is, it sounds weird but I'm really hoping it is her job that's stressing her out to the point where she has stomach cramps. I don't want to think about the possibility that Nina might be one of those people who has a terrible fate. Someone who is destined to be cut down in the prime of her life by some cruel disease.

When the cab pulls up I lean over and whisper in Nina's ear that after the fare we'll have precisely thirteen thousand, six hundred and fifty-three dollars and forty cents left to spend how we like. I get a smile and a slap on the leg.

'You're a bloody idiot. But I love you.'

Then she snuggles into my shoulder and I get her smell. And I swear it's times like that I feel like getting up off the side of the road and sprinting after that goddamn bus of happiness.

Chapter fourteen
Psycho Captain Haddock

We hit the sack as soon as we get home. Nina's out like a light but I'm too hyped-up to sleep. I'm sitting up in bed smoking a cigarette in the dark and thinking about the money. I'd forgotten what it's like to have ready cash. It's been a while.

It's not like I never had a job. It's just that I haven't had one for about two years. I used to do what Neen does—work in a service station. It was the first thing we found out we had in common. Only difference was that I worked night shifts. It totally messed with my sleep patterns. That's why I quit. Well, that and the big sweaty bearded freak. The goddamn time bomb. He's probably still out there now, ticking away. I don't care anymore, as long as he's not about to explode anywhere near me.

That's what it felt like in those days, in the early hours of the morning when he used to lean across my counter, silently demanding his packet of smokes. He came in maybe twice a week, stinking like garbage and looking like shit. He had a huge overgrown haircut and a beard like a wild black hedge. He puffed and panted and dripped sweat as if the sun was mercilessly beating down on him outside, instead of just darkness and a few flickering streetlights. He was like a giant badly dressed psycho Captain Haddock.

Every time he came in he asked for a different brand of cigarettes. And by 'asked', I mean pointed. He was either a rude prick or some kind of mute. He just stood there and pointed and occasionally grunted. And when someone's standing six feet away pointing at a great wall of cigarettes, it's almost impossible to guess which ones they want. The guy looked mean enough for starters, but you should have seen him when I didn't immediately guess which brand he wanted. He'd start rolling his eyes and grinding his teeth and grunting in frustration and rubbing his grimy fists on the counter. I'd try to get him to look at me, to help me out with some kind of sign as I rattled off the various brands in the hope of guessing the right one. His response was always to shake his head furiously, avoid eye contact and stab the air repeatedly with his left index finger. When I eventually guessed correctly he would sigh with exaggerated exasperation and unclench a sweaty crumpled twenty-dollar note from his other hand, rest his great dirty fists on the counter and fix his eyes on his cigarettes, the change and then the floor, and stomp off into the night.

I barely breathed when he was in the shop. All I thought about was finding the right pack of cigarettes and getting him out of there. It was his eyes that scared me the most. They looked unpredictable, like an angry dog's. They looked as frightened as they were frightening. And they never looked directly at me.

The first few weeks of that job were the best. I spent most of my time zoning out. Some nights I read magazines but mostly I sat alone with my thoughts, staring out past the petrol bowsers into the darkness. Staring, even though there was nothing to see. The service station wasn't on an arterial road so there was hardly any traffic. It was a fuel beacon in a dark sea of suburbia. I knew it wouldn't be too long before the sea swallowed it up altogether. I knew the day would come when I'd drive past and see a bunch of bill posters covering the joint.

After about a year of spending night after night sitting on my own, things started to get a little creepy. Maybe the nights were getting creepier, maybe it was me. Being awake and alone all night can do strange things to the brain. I don't want to sound paranoid, but while I was working there, I sometimes was. I didn't work behind a security screen or anything like that. Anyone could walk around the counter if they wanted to. And every other week the news was telling of another service station attendant who had been robbed, stabbed or shot. Or had petrol thrown over him by some junkie with a lighter and a bad case of the shakes. So as I sat there from midnight until seven a.m., I used to occasionally wonder whether it was my turn next. Whether, in fact, I had a bad fate coming to me after all. It wasn't like I thought that every person who came in was going to jump the counter with a knife and gut me. But when it was four-thirty in the morning and there were no cars on the street and when, with the radio turned off, the only sounds I could hear were my own breathing and a determined fat moth knocking against the buzzing fluoro light, I sometimes felt pretty vulnerable. Like someone could be sitting out in the darkness watching my every move.

One night I was standing behind the counter wondering how I could get on the day shift. I'd had it with nights. It wasn't just the creepy darkness or the creepy customers. My body clock was starting to sound a few alarms and anyway, I'd just met Neen and I wanted to be awake at the same times as she was.

I was snapped back from my thoughts with a great rattle of shaking steel frames. I looked up to see the psycho Captain Haddock with his enormous paw on the door handle, staring at the ground, huffing and puffing, sweat literally dripping from his beard. He looked like he was running on an exceedingly short fuse, even for him. Reluctantly, I turned off the security magnets on the main door. He immediately ripped the door open, stomped up to the counter and thrust his left index finger in the general direction of the smoke wall. The guessing game began. 'Marlboros?' I asked. He shook his head and grunted. Shit. Grunting already. I tried to speed things up. 'Peter Jacksons, mate? Winnie Blues? Escort?' He shook his head more wildly and started really stabbing the air with his index finger, grinding his teeth like a loony.

'B&H? Holidays? Jeez, bloody Alpines, mate?'

He wouldn't look at me. The grunting became growling. I guessed another wrong brand and the growling gave way to a disturbed sort of panting. Then the scary bastard muttered into the air next to him as if consulting some imaginary friend. He gave his head an almighty shake and slapped his huge palm down on the counter and let out the most blood-curdling expression of pent-up anguish I am ever likely to hear. So much for him being mute. Before I knew what was happening he'd stomped around behind the counter and he was standing six inches away from me. I was paralysed by a wave of absolute fear. My senses were overloading, taking in information about him that I hadn't picked up on before: his tracksuit pants were filthy and covered in cigarette burns; his windcheater wasn't just stained—the stain itself was still obviously wet; he stank of depravity.

I watched, petrified, motionless, as he lifted his great paw in front of my face. I was certain he was about to smack me to the floor but I was too scared to do anything about it. Then suddenly he reached right under my nose and grabbed a pouch of rolling tobacco and a packet of papers, stomped back around the other side of the counter and slammed them down. The bastard. Since when did he smoke rolling tobacco? How did he expect me to pick that one?

That wave of absolute fear had left me shaking. My mouth had gone dry. I scanned the items and tried to say the price, but I don't think I made a sound. I picked up his crumpled sweaty twenty from the counter and stuffed it in the till. He humphed and snorted like a goddamn animal when I gave him the change, then turned and stomped out of my shop.

I was about five minutes behind him. I'd had enough. I turned the pumps off and quit right then. Fuck giving two weeks' notice. The only notice I gave was the one I stuck on the door saying we were closed for the night. I sped all the way home. I don't know whether I was still scared or whether I was angry at the guy or angry at the job or angry at myself. I was in some sort of trance. The orange streetlights were whizzing overhead. Cold air was whipping in through my open window but I didn't close it. My face was freezing. It was the only part of me that felt real.

When I got home I opened a beer and I sat on the couch. I felt like a failure, throwing away my job like that. Neen had a different way of looking at it though. She reckoned it was just time to move on. At the time I didn't know what I was supposed to be moving on from. It was only later I realised that for those few years before I met her, I was either drinking and fucking all night, or working all night. If she hadn't convinced me otherwise, I would have gone and found some other night job. Or perpetual party. But she was right. It was time to move on. Time to come back to the daytime.

And right now, it's time to go to sleep. It's three o'clock in the morning and I don't know how long I've been sitting here smoking and thinking. Neen's sleeping about as soundly as she ever does. And somewhere out there, pounding the pavement under the flickering street-lights, the sweaty bearded freak's probably on his way somewhere to get another pack of cigarettes.

I feel around for the overflowing ashtray and butt out my smoke in the dark and get under the covers and snuggle up against Neen.

'Finally,' she whispers. 'Let's get some sleep.'

Chapter fifteen
The fifty-dollar vomit

I'm woken by the thud of a body landing in our bed.

It's midday. Couper's wearing a suit. 'Neen's gone to the shops,' he says. 'Then she's meeting us for lunch. Janey's coming too. It's celebration time baby!'

I don't feel like celebrating. I feel like sleeping. And why would Janey be coming out with us anyway? Couper reaches under the bed and pulls out 13,653 reasons to forget all that and just go with the flow.

'All right,' I tell him. 'But I'm not rushing anywhere.'

'We have to be at O'Connor's Riverside Restaurant at one o'clock.'

'Hey! With twenty-seven thousand bucks we can get there when we bloody well want.'

I drag myself out of bed and go and stand in front of the bathroom mirror. I'm not looking too good for a twenty-something year-old, but I'm not looking too bad either. Blotchy skin. Could do with a shave and a few sit-ups. I haven't got the time or the inclination to do sit-ups but I'll do the shave. After all, O'Connor's

Riverside Restaurant is one of the fanciest restaurants around. I want to look the part. I might even don the old suit myself. Neen would like that. So I whack on a shirt, put on the cleanest, least crumpled tie I can find and squeeze into my old pin-stripe. We're off.

Couper's brought my Dad's Kingswood over. I was supposed to return it yesterday but Couper said he wanted to keep it hidden under a tarp for twenty-four hours. Just to play safe. I think the only thing he was playing is me. He just wanted to use the bloody car himself. But I was too worried about Neen yesterday to care about Couper's latest scam. Today though, we've got to drop it back before we go to lunch. I can't see either of us being capable of driving later on. We're running late, but we still stop by the local for a quick couple of schooners. After we toast our success I find myself asking Couper why Janey's coming along today.

'I told you. I'm keeping an eye out for her at the moment.'

It strikes me as a bit weird that Couper thinks he should be keeping an eye out for Janey. She's no fool. If anything, she should be keeping an eye out for him. We knock off our beers and head back to the car. I notice he's already swapped the plates back over. I'd forgotten about that. 'Good work Couper,' I tell him.

We're at my parents' house in a matter of minutes. I give Mrs Beveringham a mighty wave as I stride up the driveway in my suit. Couper blows her a kiss. He doesn't want a grilling from my parents about how Janey's going so he takes off around the corner to wait for me.

Dad answers the door. I tell him I can't stay because I'm heading off to celebrate. He doesn't care what I'm doing, he wants to know why I didn't bring the car back yesterday. Or did I think I'd actually arranged to have it for two nights?

'Yes,' I tell him, which is sort of an answer and sort of isn't one.

'Bad chocca, Mico. Bad chocca.'

Bloody hell. I didn't know there was such a thing as bad chocca.

I was kind of hoping to be gone in under three minutes but it's not going to happen. I'm trapped on the porch until Dad finishes explaining the principle behind borrowing something from someone else. The importance of returning things on time. The sacred bond of trust between borrower and borrowee.

'Yes Dad,' I say. 'I'm sorry. I won't do it again.'

'Damn right you won't son.'

'Yeah Dad, I know. But I'm sorry anyway.'

He ends his lecture with a tear welling in his eye and the devastating news that he couldn't make it to the shops before closing yesterday to buy Mum the fresh ginger she wanted for her soup. That last night they had to eat carrot and ginger-from-the-packet soup. I leave knowing that fact, and knowing that it'll be a cold day in hell before he lends me his Kingswood again.

I meet up with Couper who's somehow managed to wangle a taxi. We get to O'Connor's Riverside Restaurant at about ten minutes past one and clatter our way through to a table where the girls are already enjoying a cold beer each.

'Two more thanks, mate,' I say to the waiter at my elbow.

'Have a fuckin' squiz at that,' says Couper. We've got a fantastic view across the river. I have a squiz and then sit down and wait for my beer, knowing I won't have to wait too long in a joint like this.

The menu makes me laugh. Amazing what some people will pay for food. There's even a bloody fifty-dollar hamburger. It's some hamburger, too. Grain-fed beef served with special coloured lettuce and some ritzy goddamn vegetables. All topped off with Tasmanian truffles. Bloody hell. Nina's having a duck glazed in some sauce I can't even pronounce. Janey's having some crazy vegetarian dish. She reckons she hasn't eaten meat for about three years. Couper's having kangaroo. 'Love a bit of road-kill,' he says. Myself, I reckon I'll have a crack at that fifty-dollar burger.

We're drinking imported beers only. I know we haven't won a million bucks or anything so we can't go overboard, but I reckon it might be good to splurge today and get it out of our system. Nina agrees but says that after we pay the bill, I can keep five hundred dollars and she's in charge of the rest. No questions asked. I clink her glass and nod in agreement and we settle back to enjoy the day. Couper's in fine form. He's telling horror stories from the funeral parlour and even some of the people around us are eating silently and listening in to what really goes on at those places.

They're not your average stories but then again, we're not your average posh restaurant clientele. Couper challenges me to scull my beer and so I do—without realising the bastard's tipped a whole shaker of salt into it. I last about a second before what I think is going to be a cough turns out to be a mild vomit. I choke a hunk of chewed burger down my front and spit some partially digested truffles onto the tablecloth, but manage to retain most of it in my mouth. It tastes so disgusting that I have to go and throw up properly in the bathroom. When I get back to the table Couper is still laughing. I think Janey wants to but she's holding back. Nina's pissed off. 'It's a bloody waste of money, Mico. What's the point of eating a fifty-dollar burger if it's just going to end up in the toilet ten minutes later?'

I know it's a waste. I tell her it wasn't my fault, it was Couper.

'Ah, ten minutes, two hours. What's the difference?' he says.

Janey covers the mess on the table with some serviettes. The stain on my tie seems to blend in all right with the original design. Nina asks me if I'm going to spew again.

'No. All done.' I thump my chest once and give a final burp.

Couper giggles and Nina tries to scowl but breaks into a smile. 'Okay,' she says to Couper, 'but try that again and I'll reach down your throat and pull that fuckin' road-kill back out—got it?'

Couper nods meekly, cheekily, and orders another round before we have dessert and everything's okay again.

Neen's not feeling too bad she reckons. She's working out how much notice to give Mick the prick. Couper reckons she should keep quiet and wait for the busiest shift of the week and then not turn up. Leave him facing his own endless queue of twenty people. Neen says no way. I knew it. She doesn't work like that. And she doesn't quit work like that either.

So we keep sitting there all afternoon because we can. We can afford it and so we can afford to enjoy it. The only down side is that we can't smoke in the restaurant, no matter how much Couper offers to bribe the waiter. So me and Couper are standing outside, smoking, when we notice the paddleboats. I only have to look at him to know we're thinking the same thing. We go back inside where the girls are working their way through two cocktails each at once. I've not seen Nina this drunk for a while. At any rate, she's drunk enough to agree to go for a ride on the river. Janey's keen as well. 'Just try not to hit any parked paddleboats,' she tells Couper as she pokes him in the ribs.

'Cheeky bloody girl,' he smiles.

To our waiters' relief, we pay the bill and get out of

there. Nina makes sure we leave a decent tip. Couper tells the waiter 'get a fuckin' haircut'.

The paddleboats guy is only about fifteen and he thinks it's a bit of a lark that we're going out when we're so plastered. He says we've got an hour and points us in the direction of a big fountain in the middle of the river. 'Go and have a shower if you like,' he grins, knowing we're so pissed that we probably will, suits and all.

So we climb into the boats. Me and Nina are in red paddleboat number seven and Couper and Janey are in green paddleboat number nine. There's not much room. Me and Neen are almost sitting on top of each other. It's not very comfortable but I soon forget about it when Nina steers us under the fountain. The water is freezing cold and it stinks. Nina throws back her head laughing and holds out her arms. 'Oh my god! Don't you feel so alive?'

I don't know about feeling alive. Mainly I feel wet, but I also feel good when I see her so happy like that. More than good. Bloody great, actually.

I grab her hand and we paddle away from the fountain and then we lay back and soak up the sun. We close our eyes and put our feet up and hold hands and wait for our livers and our clothes to dry out. I can feel the sun warming my eyelids and it feels so good I don't think I'll ever want to open them again.

But I do. And I look at Neen lying there, eyes closed, smiling, wet in the sun. Her t-shirt clinging to her belly. I put my hand on her wet t-shirt belly. 'You okay today?'

'Yeah. Good today.'

'Shall we go see a doctor soon, anyway?'

'Maybe.'

Maybe's a start. I lie back and shut my eyes again and enjoy the sun's warmth. After a couple of minutes I start dropping off to sleep but the sound of Janey laughing rouses me just before I reach the point of no return. I open my weary eyes to see Couper standing up in his paddleboat next to us holding what looks like a bucket full of dirty river water and wearing an even dirtier grin on his face. 'G'day Mico,' he smiles.

Chapter sixteen
Ain't no fuckin' Snowtown

I decide to walk home. It'll take about an hour but it will give me a chance to dry off. Couper nailed me good and proper. Don't know where he got the bucket from but he always manages to turn something up when he needs it. Neen didn't get a drop on her. Had a good laugh though. She offered to walk home with me but I don't mind going on my own.

The day's getting on. It's already getting dark and the streets are empty. I look up ahead to see a couple of fellas sitting on the gutter. It looks like they're drinking bottles of beer but I can't be sure on such a poorly lit street. When I get near enough, one of them asks me for a light. I look at him. Even under the low glow of the streetlight his weather-beaten face seems unusually red. He looks pretty rough around the edges. In fact, he could be pretty damn mean-looking if he tried, but he looks friendly right now. And he wants a light.

'Sure,' I say. 'Here you go.'

'Thanks buddy.'

I ask why the two of them are sitting on the side of the road with a carton of beer. Redface points with his lit cigarette to the bus stop. I hadn't noticed it. He hands me back my lighter.

'You can fuck off now,' says the other bloke. He's quite a bit smaller than Redface. His short little legs don't even appear to stretch out half as much. But his face looks like it could be equally as mean. And his tone of voice suggests he's a man who's never let his height stop him from winning a fight. I'm a little surprised by his curtness. Redface leans back and has a great old chuckle, obviously enjoying the smaller guy's rudeness. Somehow though, in spite of the small guy's menacing tone of voice, Redface's hearty laugh, coupled with the afternoon's beer makes me feel surprisingly relaxed.

'Jeez,' I say, playfully. 'That's a little harsh mate.'

'Yeah, Tiny,' says Redface. 'A little harsh. C'mon man, the brother gave me a light.'

He's agreeing with me but I can't help feel he's mocking me just a little bit as well. Tiny looks up, shakes his head slightly and stares at me. He doesn't change his expression but I get a sense he's uneasy. Redface reaches down and grabs a bottle from the open carton. 'Wanna beer?' he says. Without waiting for an answer he pulls a bottle opener from his jacket pocket and flips the cap off.

'Nice opener,' I say. It's got a curved pointy bit on the end so you can punch holes in the tops of cans.

Redface holds out the beer for me. I kind of want to keep walking and get back to Neen, but I don't feel like being bad-mannered so I say thanks and take it.

Redface tells me not to worry about Tiny. That he was just being a rude prick. I try to remain confident without being arrogant. I don't want these fellas to think they intimidate me, even though, if I wasn't a little bit pissed still, they probably would. I say, 'Yeah, well nothing wrong with a rude prick now and then,' and I give Tiny a wink. He gives me a quick half-smile as if to say 'you're all right mate'. I suppose he could have just as easily been saying 'you're a dickhead mate'. Hard to tell with some people.

So I'm there on the side of the road with these two strange blokes who've asked for a light and offered me a beer. There's not really anywhere to go from here, but now that we're sharing a beer together, I feel I have to say something. There seems to be some tension between us. Perhaps I appeared too confident too quickly. I don't know. All I know is that nobody's saying much. It's become a bit of a poker game. I think they're trying to guess my hand. I don't like the silence and so I lay my first bet.

'So, what's up then?'

Tiny doesn't answer me. I take a big gulp of beer and then Redface says, 'Whaddaya mean "what's up"?' I don't like the tone of his voice. It's short and dismissive. And to be honest, it pisses me off. I mean, why offer a bloke a beer if you're just going to sit there and snap at him like that? Tiny's not even looking at me. He's staring down at the ground drawing a line in the dirt or something. It's almost as if he's waiting for something to happen. But so am I. I'm waiting for a goddamn decent conversation.

'I mean: so what do you know?'

There's a bit of challenge in my voice. Redface looks up, pauses. Just when I start thinking he's not even going to answer me, he says what he knows is that he got out of jail earlier today. 'If that's all right with you,' he says sardonically.

If the conversation's a poker game, he's raised the stakes somewhat. I wasn't expecting that one, nor do I have anything to say that will raise him. I've got the option to chuck in my hand and change the subject, but for some reason I decide to see him instead. I ask him what he was in for. He says he got caught with a paedophile locked in his shed. Doesn't say anything else, just that he got caught with a paedophile locked in his shed. And stares right past me.

I wonder exactly what he means. I wonder whether it was someone who abused him, or someone who abused his kids. I wonder whether he had someone locked in his shed for three hours or three weeks. I wonder whether the paedophile might have even been dead. I give a bit of a nervous laugh. 'Fuck, mate. That's a bit Snowtown isn't it?'

Redface looks up. 'Mate, it ain't no fucking Snowtown,' he sneers. By the tone of that sneer I can tell that I ain't his fucking mate either.

The more I look at the man, the more I start to think that he looks a bit dangerous. Possibly a lot dangerous. I start to wonder how long he has just spent in jail. And then I realise I don't want to know. I want to chuck in my hand now. I want to fold. The stakes are getting too high. I'm beginning to see a look in Redface's eye that I hadn't seen before. A look of anger and fear and pain rolled into one. His hearty laugh seems far away now. Almost like it belonged to another man. I start wishing I'd fucked off when Tiny told me to.

I try to make a clean exit. 'Anyway, I think I might be on my way now lads.'

'Where the fuck do you think you're going?' says Redface suddenly. It's as if my leaving has just snapped him awake. And he's suddenly speaking with a tone so sharp that it could slice through a man's neckbone. I'm rattled. Still, I try to answer as if I'm not fazed. I keep my poker-face. 'Just heading home, mate.'

Redface heaves himself to his feet and comes so close we're almost touching. He's taller than I would have thought, or hoped.

'The fuck you are,' he hisses.

He's calling my bluff. But suddenly cards are the furthest thing from my mind.

'You snotty little cunt. What was I in for? What the fuck is it to you what I was in for?'

I can smell the booze on his breath. It reeks. I didn't realise how drunk he was. I shouldn't be surprised though.

I mean, who can blame him for getting loaded on his first night out of the joint? I only have myself to blame for asking him stupid questions.

'Sorry man. I didn't mean anything by it. Look, why don't I just go now?' I look down at Tiny, who rolls his eyes at me. 'I told you to fuck off before, you dumb cunt,' he sighs and gets to his feet. He's a good two foot shorter than his mate.

'Sidown Tiny!' roars Redface. 'This cunt ain't going fucking nowhere! Fucking nowhere!' He whips the bottle opener from his jacket pocket and presses the pointy end into the side of my throat. He grabs my chin in his other hand. It's a gentle grip but I feel more trapped than if he had my chin in a vice. He looks me dead in the eye. 'I'll fucking kill you motherfucker,' he says quietly. He twists the opener so that the pointed end grips into loose skin. 'I'll rip a hole in your fucking throat. Don't think I won't, you little cunt.'

I don't think that he won't. In fact I'm starting to really think that he will. I glance over at Tiny and I'm glad to see he hasn't sat back down. But he's not exactly rushing to help me either. I can't believe he's so calm.

'Come on man,' he says to Redface. 'Leave him go. The brother gave you a light, remember?'

I'm relieved to hear that he's trying to defuse the situation. I'm just beginning to wish he was a little taller. But I underestimate the man. Somehow, he eases himself between us and I feel the skin on my neck untwist a little

143

as Redface is forced to step back. His eyes are looking over Tiny's shoulder, daring me to make a run for it. Pinning me to the spot. I can feel his voice in my stomach.

'I wanna fuckin' kill the little cunt,' he says, about me, while he looks me in the eye.

'No you don't, mate. No you don't,' says Tiny. 'Let's wait for the bus and then go home and drink some more of them beers.'

He looks back over his shoulder at me and says in an unbelievably friendly voice, 'Okay then buddy, we'll catch up with you later on.' Then he starts talking to Redface and trying to distract him. I take the hint and start to quietly back away.

'Where the fuck do you think you're going?' shouts Redface. 'Fucking Snowtown! I'll give you fucking Snowtown you little cunt! I'll put you in a fucking barrel!'

I grit my teeth and ignore him and hope. The last thing I see before I turn my back is a determined Tiny doing his best to restrain the raging man who seems twice his size. Somehow he's managing. I listen to Redface screaming murderous threats until I decide I'm far enough away and then I start running as fast as I can.

They say it doesn't matter how much coffee or water you drink. They say it doesn't matter if you go for a long walk. They say you can't dull the effects of alcohol any faster than the body can process it. After my run-in with Redface and Tiny I know that's bullshit. You can get scared sober.

Neen's still awake when I get home. It's later than I thought it was. She's not drunk anymore. She's sitting on the couch having a cup of tea and watching telly. When I walk in the room she turns the telly off. 'You took your time didn't you? What happened?' She sounds pissed off. I shrug and my neck suddenly stings so I reach up to touch it. It's wet. I look at my finger. There's blood on it.

Nina jumps up off the couch and takes my hand and looks at my finger and then my neck. 'Oh, Mico,' she says. 'What happened?'

Chapter seventeen
The clown

In the morning I feel pretty seedy and pretty stupid and pretty lucky to even be around. My neck hurts. It's got an elastoplast strip on it now. Nina comes into the bedroom with a coffee. She tells me I can share it as she puts it on the bedside table and climbs back under the doona. I lean over her and slurp from the top of the mug and then snuggle my hot wet coffee moustache against her back. We lie there quietly for a few minutes listening to each other breathe. By that, I really do mean listening to each other breathe. We both had too many cigarettes yesterday so the mucus traffic in our lungs makes for some pretty gravelly exhalations.

Nina rips back the doona. 'Dammit. I'm hungry. I'm gonna get some toast.' She hops out of bed and I roll over into her warmish void and pull the doona over my head. Ah, the smell of Nina. The phone rings. I reach outside the doona and drag it back under.

It's Janey. 'So are you guys still coming?'

'Coming where?'

'To the circus, of course. Go on, you promised you'd come with us.'

Apparently yesterday we organised with Janey and Couper to go and sit on the city museum lawns and watch one of her tennis students performing in a kids' circus.

'Um ... yeah ... of course. We're on our way.'

Janey says that after the circus she's going to speak to her teachers about going back to school. I tell her that it sounds like a good plan.

'Yeah,' she says. 'It was Couper's idea. So we'll see you on the museum lawns then?'

'Half an hour.'

I hang up as a hand reaches in under the doona. I smell vegemite and I take a hot buttery piece of toast in my mouth.

'Fanks Meen.'

'Move over. I don't want your crumbs on my side of the bed.'

Twenty minutes or so later we're on a train into town. I'm so hungover my muscles ache. We have to swap carriages twice because I feel myself getting panicky. It's the noise and the activity and the people all around that set it off. In the end I stick my fingers in my ears and shut my eyes until Neen tells me we're pulling into the city.

We get to the museum lawns fifteen minutes late, but we're lucky—if you can call it that. Couper and Janey are waving frantically from the audience and it looks like they've saved seats for us. I don't like the look of where they are. Right in the middle of the crowd, up on the third level of some makeshift scaffolding. Goddamn it. I'm feeling strung out enough without sitting squashed up there. But I don't have much choice so we climb up and squeeze past a row of knees to our seats.

'Hi Mico. Hi Neen,' whispers Janey. She sounds excited and I give her a smile. I'm sitting between her and Nina. Couper is sitting next to Janey on the other side. For some strange reason he and Janey are holding hands. He must see the puzzled look on my face because he lets go of Janey's hand and offers me a handshake.

'Hey man,' he whispers.

'Hey,' I whisper back and shake his hand. We haven't shaken hands like that for years. It's like he's introducing himself to me for the first time. On his best behaviour or something. I look at him staring at me with a big genuine smile on his face. Genuine smiles don't really suit Coups. They make him look creepy. I look at Janey. She's smiling too. And now she's got her hand on Couper's leg. And then it hits me—that's what we're here for. Not the bloody kids' circus, but for the Couper and Janey show.

Bloody hell. Couper and Janey together. I don't know whether it bothers me or not. I can't help feeling Couper's a bit old for her. He's twenty-fuckin'-eight after all. When the two of them turn their smiley faces to the stage I whisper to Neen, 'Did you know about this?'

'They were kissing in the paddleboats yesterday,' she whispers back. 'Isn't it cute?'

'Isn't he a bit old?'

'Shhh.'

Janey taps my leg and points at the kids on stage. 'Look, Mico.'

'So which one's your student?'

She points out a girl hanging upside-down three metres in the air from a rope using her legs only. The girl is almost completely exposed up there in her white leotard. She's got her whole body on display. She hasn't got breasts yet and her waist and groinal area are pokey and awkward like the various bones are growing at different speeds. She looks gangly, just like a kid should. I have to admit, she looks nothing like Janey.

I look over at Couper. He's got a sparkle in his eye. A sparkle more happy than wicked. He's got a kind, childish face when he's not looking wicked. He looks younger than his twenty-eight years. And he bloody well acts like it sometimes. I dunno. I suppose he and Janey might meet somewhere in the middle. I shrug and settle back to watch the other show.

It's pretty amazing stuff. There's a goddamn ten-year-old kid walking the tightrope. The cheeky little bastard even manages to lie down and pretend he's having a kip. There's a kid clown who gets around the stage by walking on top of a rolling ball and another kid riding a unicycle bigger than he is. It's impressive stuff. And it's pretty goddamn enjoyable. For a while that is.

It's a hot day and the longer I sit and watch from

the scaffolding, the more uncomfortable I become. I start feeling like the audience is closing in on me. I can feel myself getting a little nervous, and my chest starting to tighten. It's nothing drastic but I know that once I start feeling a little edgy, a full-blown freak-out might be just around the corner. That once I start feeling a little bit dizzy, I'm liable to pass out. I don't want anything bad to happen here. I'm surprisingly happy watching the kids' circus with my recently united sister and best friend. I'm trying to be anyway. If I can just go for a quick walk and stretch my legs I'll be okay. But my breathing's getting more rapid and I'm starting to sweat. I shift in my seat. Neen puts a reassuring hand on my knee. She knows what's going on.

Janey doesn't. 'Are you okay?'

I nod but I can't bring myself to speak and I know I'm unconvincing. She looks down at my hands which have started shaking slightly.

'You're having a panic attack aren't you?'

How Janey guesses that, I have no idea.

'It's okay,' she says quietly. 'You told me about them at one of Couper's parties. You probably don't remember.'

She'd be right there.

'Just concentrate on your breathing,' she whispers. 'The show only goes for about another ten minutes and then we can get out of here and go for a walk. I'll go and speak with the teachers another day.'

'Okay,' I say. But it's not. I'm trying to concentrate on my breathing but I can't. I feel like I want to scream but

I know I'll feel like a fool if I do. I hold on as long as I can and then I whisper, 'I've got to go.'

Neen nods. 'Okay.'

Janey hears and says that they'll go too. Couper nods his head and gets up to leave. I don't actually care who comes and who stays. I just know I have to get out of the crowd. I start squeezing back out past the row of knees but then I hear a whispered 'fuck' and so I glance over my shoulder. Couper looks unsteady. The poor bastard must have tripped on his shoelace or something. He's teetering like a nervous skydiver about to jump. Only he's not in a plane, he's in the middle of a packed crowd sitting bunched together on three levels of scaffolding.

At least, he is for two more seconds.

The look on his face as he sails over the oblivious people below him is as close to a look of pure dread as I've ever seen Couper give. It's the most un-cheeky I've ever seen the man and it's enough to snap me out of my own state of panic into a state of amused sympathy. I'm not sure though, who I should feel more sorry for— my best mate, or the unfortunate old gentleman in the front row with the bald head. A head which seems to be an organic magnet for Couper's own shaven skull.

The sound of two hairless craniums colliding is one I will never forget. It's sharp yet hollow, and it resonates pain. Makes me wince. I almost expect to see two grey-matter yolks pouring out of those great big pink hard-boiled eggs. Grandpa goes bony-arse-up onto the stage in front of him, taking the unicycle kid out on the way. About three seconds later Couper bobs his head up from the front of the crowd. I didn't think it was possible but he looks even less cheeky than before. He actually looks embarrassed. I've never seen Couper look embarrassed and I can't help cracking a smile. The mums and dads in the audience have started clicking their tongues like machine-guns, shooting him down where he stands.

Someone helps Grandpa to his feet. He's shaken but he's all right. Probably taken harder knocks in his time. The same can't be said for the unicycle kid. Poor little bloke's got scratches on his knees and he's bawling like the eight-year-old he probably is. Still, he'll be all right in a minute. I can already see at least three mums going to his rescue. And I suppose we'll have to go and rescue Couper.

We push our way out through a forty-knee turnstile, smothering our giggles and shaking our heads in a show of disapproval. It's no use though. The audience already hates us. We've been tarred with Couper's brush. It's as if we pushed him. We get to the front of the stage, grab Couper and leg it around the side of the museum. He looks completely stunned. He's rubbing his forehead. Janey's trying to help him rub but she's laughing too hard to concentrate properly.

'Richard,' she snorts. 'You fucking clown.'

Couper starts to chuckle. And then the chuckle becomes a laugh and he leans an elbow on Janey's shoulder and an elbow on mine. And Neen starts to laugh too. And we hang out in that side alley by the museum and laugh and laugh. And then I hear someone else's laugh joining in. It's a familiar one. I look down towards the sound and there's bloody Eric Papadopoulos sitting in his wheelchair. And when I catch my breath I slap him on the back and ask him what the hell he's doing here.

Chapter eighteen
Goooooooooooo*aaaaaa*ll!!

I should have guessed, Eric was watching his little brother. Warren Papadopoulos was in the kids' circus—he was the clown walking around on top of that ball. Multi-talented little bastard.

'Sorry Mico?' says Couper. 'Does he have another talent?'

Eric grins. 'Watch it,' he says, and then asks us whether we want to go somewhere for a beer. Of course we do. So Eric goes and finds Cass and then we all head to our usual beer garden.

Ever since the robbery, Couper has had at least three grand on him at any one time. He loves flicking through his stash of fifties, even if he's only shelling out two goddamn bucks for something. So he brings out a wad of cash while he's getting the first round. Eric looks stunned. 'What'd you do?' he says to Couper. 'Rob a bank or something?' Couper gives him a wink and a smile and gets a sharp elbow from Janey.

Eric turns to me. 'Bloody hell, Mico, I can't believe

you and Nina ended up going out again after that van crash. Hadn't you had enough for one night?'

I tell him we were drunk enough for it to seem like the best idea at the time.

'Anyway, what ended up happening to you?' Cass says to Couper. Couper tells the short version of how he probably won't be driving anymore, legally at least, for quite a while. Eric says maybe that's a good thing. Says we were all pretty lucky that night. Couper's not convinced.

'You call that lucky? Getting busted?'

'Shit mate, getting caught's nothing. I mean, bloody hell, Couper. You're lucky it didn't turn out worse. You could have bloody well ended up like me.'

Couper takes a sip of his beer. 'You're not so bad off,' he says. 'You still got your girl and your sport and your beer and—' he pauses and smiles cheekily '—your little brother to sing to you if you ever need a good laugh.'

'Oi! Smart-arse!' Eric starts punching shit out of Couper's right leg. Couper yells in pain and jumps out of his seat to avoid the blows. Eric points at him. 'Just count yourself lucky you can feel anything at all, you fuckin' idiot.' He's smiling now but you can tell he's still serious.

I get up to buy a round. When I get back the subject's been changed. The others hardly even look up as I plonk the beers down. They're too busy trying to work out what's more difficult—walking a tightrope or balancing on a ball. Couper says the rope. Cass says the ball. Eric grins and says they'd be about as hard as each other, he reckons. Neen looks like she doesn't give a shit. I don't either. We slip into our own conversation. I ask her how she's feeling and she says a bit crook. She doesn't look great. I talk in a low voice so as not to break up the tightrope/ball banter. I tell her I'm making an appointment for the gynaecologist in the morning, whether she likes it or not.

'Ha,' she laughs, quietly. 'Sure you will. Go on then.'

'What's that s'posed to mean?'

'You won't remember in the morning, Mico. You never do.'

'Bullshit. I wouldn't forget something as important as that.'

'Bullshit yourself.' She's not arguing mad. She's arguing amused. 'What about last week? You were going to make an appointment last week.'

'Bullshit. When?'

'And the week before that. And the week before that. And the week before that.'

'Bullshit.'

'It's okay,' she smiles. 'I don't want to go anyway. I hate fuckin' doctors. I just wish you'd stop carrying on like you're the big responsible partner or something. I wish you'd stop telling me to look after myself. You should just worry about you, okay honey?'

I'm stuck somewhere between indignation and wanting to see the funny side along with her. I mean, she's probably got a point. But still, I can prove her wrong.

'You mark my words Nina Kartiniski. I am making you an appointment tomorrow, whether—'

'Sure, do whatever you like,' she sighs. 'And we'll deal with tomorrow tomorrow. But one thing at a time. I'm going to go to bed as soon as we get home. I'm worn out. Could you do me a favour later?'

'Anything.'

'Could you leave the lights off when you come to bed?'

'Sure thing,' I say. 'No lights.'

Coups tries to drag us back into the conversation. 'What do you reckon, Neen? Tightrope or ball?'

Neen smiles and says sorry but no matter how hard she tries she just can't make herself give a shit. Either way, she says, there's no doubting that Warren Papadopoulos is an extremely talented young man. Couper snorts and bites his tongue and Janey smacks him on the arm. Then Couper stretches his smacked arm around Janey. They sort of catch themselves and look at me. I raise my glass and tell them 'cheers'.

Eric says that his little brother isn't the only Papadopoulos who knows a trick or two. Cass groans. 'Here we go. What is it now, show-off?'

'I think he's going to start another fight,' says Couper.

Eric ignores both of them and wheels himself away from the table. The far side of the beer garden has a kind of footpath ramp-thing that winds around down to the main bar. The near side has the option of a short-cut couple of steps. Six steps, in fact. Eric goes to the top of the stairs.

'Eric,' says Cass. 'What the fuck do you think you're doing?'

'Going for the record, Cassy. Going for the big six.'

Before Cass can protest he's already rocked back on his rear wheels and bounced down to the first step. I say 'bounced', but it's more like a precise slow-motion drop. Then a hold. He's like a cyclist at traffic lights with his feet strapped to the pedals, trying not to keel over. Only there's much more risk in what he's doing. He really could come a cropper. He can't lower his front wheels at all. There's not enough room. He has to regain his balance on each step before he attempts to drop to the next one. And he has to make it to the bottom on his own, upright or not. It would be too hard for me and Couper to lean over the railing and haul him out of the chair, even if we weren't so beery.

'Oh, Eric,' sighs Cass. 'You are a fucking idiot, boy.' She looks around the table for moral support. You get the feeling she's seen him do this one too many times. But *we* haven't. So there's no moral support coming from us just yet; we all want to see whether he makes it or not. To be honest, I don't like the man's chances. Especially seeing as he's had a few beers. I don't reckon I could walk down those steps at a brisk pace right now and not miss a beat. But he's taking it on, step by step. Slowly but surely. Ignoring the grumbling arseholes who have to walk over to the other side of the beer garden and go the long way around on the ramp.

He takes an especially long time on the last step. Perhaps for effect. Or maybe he's just making sure he gets it right. Whatever, he lands the final bounce and sets his front wheels down and lets out a huge cry. 'Papadopouloooooooooooooooos!' he yells, holding his powerful arms in the air like a heavyweight champion. 'Gooooooooooooaaaaaall!'

'Did he say goal?' asks Couper. 'What the fuck's "goal" got to do with it?'

'Keep your mouth shut,' I say. 'Or he might chuck you down those bloody steps.'

Eric's yelling 'goal' all the way as he wheels himself back to join us at the table. He helps himself to a big drink of beer. 'Let's see those fuckin' circus kids do that.'

And so the afternoon goes on and we have a few more beers and eventually Couper brings out his wad and bets Eric fifty bucks he can't do the stair thing again. Cass threatens to leave if he tries, so Couper settles for betting Eric that he can't stay balanced on his two back wheels while sculling a whole pint of beer. Technically, by agreeing to such a challenge Eric demonstrates that he doesn't exactly need a pint of beer at this point but nevertheless, Couper manages to get the bet up and running.

Although it's a difficult task, everyone, even Cass, seems confident he can pull it off after already witnessing his stair prowess. And he does. For about five seconds. And then almost faster than I can see, Eric Papadopoulos is flat on his back soaked in his own beer and half whimpering, half laughing, 'Goooooooaaaaalll.'

The wheelchair's lying on its side and Eric's magazines and his empty coke bottle and jumper and spare catheters have all spilt out.

'Fuck,' he says. 'I'm pissed. Couper, give us a hand getting back into that thing will ya?'

'Sure, but first you owe me fifty bucks.'

Eric snorts and reaches into his shirt pocket and pulls out a fifty which he hands to Couper. I shove Eric's stuff back in his wheelchair bag and we right the chair and help him into it. He's a heavy bastard.

'We'd better go now,' sighs Cass. 'We've got to check whether he's cut himself anywhere, anyway.'

'Yeah,' manages Eric. 'Got ta bloody well check.'

'Nice doing business with ya,' smiles Couper, adding the new fifty to his wad.

Cass and Eric say goodbye and take off down the ramp.

'We should get going too,' says Neen. 'You guys have had it.'

Then someone says, 'Richard Couper. We'd like a word with you.'

We look up to see two stout men in suits. Couper looks down at the wad of fifties in his hand and then up at one of the men, who is holding out his badge.

'Would you like a daiquiri, Detective?' he says.

Chapter nineteen
What are you gonna do?

There's nothing on telly and I'm bored stiff. Nina's gone to bed. The two of us left the beer garden while Couper was still attempting to convince two pissed-off detectives to try a cocktail. We got out of there pretty quick. I didn't want to chance the detectives questioning me as well. But now that I'm home, I'm not tired and the last thing I feel like doing is sitting around. For some reason, I get it into my head to go and visit my dad in his front bar. As it would happen, now is probably not a bad time to do it. I've got most of my five hundred dollars left. Maybe I'll even do a bit of a Couper and splash some cash around.

I don't wake Neen to tell her. Anyway, I might not be gone long. I'm not even sure that Dad's going to be there. I think about giving him a ring to check, but it'll be far more satisfying walking in there if he doesn't know I'm coming. I can just see the look on his face. Maybe he'll even say, 'G'day mate', and pause his conversation with someone else and turn side-on to them and start talking to me. If he's there, that is. And if he's not? Well,

I'll just get some take-aways and go back home and think of something else to do.

It's just after dinner time when I get to Dad's front bar. My stomach grumbles. I think maybe I should have had some food on the way. I look around. Bob the butcher's watching the last dog race up on the TV. There are a few other blokes standing around with schooners but my dad's not one of them. I know I said if he wasn't here that I'd go and get some take-aways but there's always the chance he might turn up in a minute so I decide to order a bowl of hot chips and sit it out for a while. I get a pint of beer to pass the time and I light a fag and check out the plaques and trophies hanging behind my dad's front bar. I get my second pint before the chips arrive. And when they do I'm shovelling them so fast into my face that I barely pay attention to the voice behind me.

'Hey, you're Milo's boy aren't you?'

'Milo?' I turn and look. It's Bob the butcher.

'Yeah ... um ... Stan's boy aren't you? Stan Millevic?'

I'm pretty pleased to be recognised. 'Sure am. I'm Mico. Want a drink?'

'She's right mate,' says Bob. But I bring out my little stash of fifty dollar notes and buy him an imperial pint of Caffrey's because I remember I saw him drinking one last time I was here.

'Steady on, boy,' he says when I hand it to him.

'You drink this stuff don't you?'

'Yeah, but only when I have a bit of a win on the gee-gees.' He looks down and sees the fifties in my hand. 'Like you must have.'

I tell him this particular windfall was from hard work and not luck and that, anyway, money is just money to me and an imperial pint of Caffrey's for a friend of my dad's is no sweat. Bob says he thought I was unemployed.

'Was,' I lie but I don't go on and he doesn't ask me to.

The chips give me a second wind and Bob's quite good company so I sit there with him for a while longer. He's got stories like you wouldn't believe about the people in our neighbourhood. If Beveringham's the eyes, then Bob the butcher's the ears. He remembers every little bit of gossip he hears about people and he's not afraid to pass it on. He even reckons he's got a couple of good stories about my dad. He won't tell me though. 'If he wanted you to know he would have already told you himself,' he says.

Not bloody likely, I think.

Bob's going on about some new guy who's just moved to the neighbourhood. Some fat guy called Avery Mollison. Reckons he's bad news. Reckons he got fingered for being a flasher in Tea Tree Gully but they could never pin it on him. I ask him if he reckons I should maybe warn my little sister.

'Maybe,' he says. 'You never know with those sorts of blokes. Speaking of which, how's Jessop's backhand going? Or was it his forehand? Or was it both hands?'

Then he leans back and finishes off his glass of Caffrey's and has a big laugh. When Bob the butcher says it like that it sounds funny so I laugh too and then I buy him another pint. He tells me to steady on. Tells me not to spend all my hard-earned money at once.

'Don't worry Bob,' I wink. 'There's plenty more where that came from.'

Then I tell him I'm going to get that Mr Jessop one day. I tell him I've got my own grudge against dirty old bastards. A couple of other regulars start milling around and pretty soon I'm shouting everyone drinks and telling them loudly and clearly how there should be much heavier punishments for sexual abuse. Someone agrees with me and I agree back louder and I keep talking about dirty old men and suddenly I'm telling everyone about how I sucked on Aaron's cock that time and about how I accidentally tore my hairdresser's fishnet stockings and about how I got the blow job from the deaf guy near the train station. The barmaid's nodding her head patiently and Bob the butcher's sitting there with eyebrows raised and the couple of regulars aren't saying so much anymore. They all seem to be waiting for me to finish. And when I finish whatever the hell I was saying, Bob the butcher says he has to head off now but it sure was interesting to meet Stan Millevic's son.

'Nice to meet you too,' I slur and then I look around for the regulars but they seem to have wandered off. The barmaid's taken my glass and I don't think my dad's going to come in so I decide I may as well go and get some take-aways and get myself home. But I forget about the take-aways before I'm outside the door. I forget about doing anything except going home to get some sleep.

When I wake up in the morning I remember some things. I remember with a smile that Bob the butcher recognised me. I remember those hot chips tasted damn nice. Then I cringe for a full minute when I remember that I told my sordid sexual history to Dad's front bar pals. I also remember I basically paid for everyone's drinks all night, which would explain why I only have four fifties left.

Damn it. It's probably not my best ever effort. Probably I should have stayed home. I don't beat myself up about it too much though. I mean, what are ya gonna do? I know what *I'm* going to do. I'm going to make that goddamn appointment for Neen. And then I'm going to lie in bed until I can bring myself to go and get a couple of beers to take the edge off the afternoon.

Chapter twenty
Not totally fucked up right now

Those detectives would have tracked Couper down sooner except that he'd been 'honeymooning' with Janey at the Hyatt under a false name. I should have guessed he'd do something like that. It's typical Couper. Enjoying the fruits of his labour. Anyway, he ended up going down to the police station with them, even though he didn't have to. They questioned him for an hour or so, but like Couper says, you can question a man all you like but you can't arrest him for having a good run on the dogs—whether you believe him or not. Even so, before they let him go, one of the detectives told Couper it was in his best interests not to leave town for a while. I don't know what they expect to turn up. They already searched Couper's house and didn't find any more money. And they didn't find any more money in the honeymoon suite at the Hyatt either. I wonder what he's done with his share. Maybe he's just spent it.

So Couper's okay for now which means I sort of am too. I do wonder though if the two detectives thought I might have left in a bit of a rush the other day. Whether they're going to start checking me out as well. I wonder whether they'd turn anything up if they started sniffing about. Like when I was flashing my cash around the other night with Bob the butcher. I was so pissed I can't even be completely sure that I didn't tell him about the robbery. Surely I didn't? Surely I wasn't that stupid?

'Surely,' I say out loud to myself. Neen glances up from her magazine and frowns but she doesn't say anything. We're in a waiting room. Neen's waiting to see the gynae-cologist and I'm waiting for Neen to say something. She hasn't spoken since we got here. I guess maybe she just doesn't feel like talking. Maybe that's how it is when you're a twenty-seven-year-old woman in a gynaecologist's waiting room.

'You stupid, stupid bastards. You won't get away with it.'

Or maybe not.

'Now come on Neen—'

'Don't "come on" me. You and Couper are stupid bastards and I knew you'd get caught.'

'Shhh.' Crikey. I'd rather she started ranting on about some massive boil on my nuts than the bloody robbery at this volume. I drop my voice to a whisper. 'Look, nobody's been caught. They're just carrying out an investigation. Couper will be fine. They've got nothing on him except that he's come into some money recently. He'll just keep telling them he had a few wins on the dogs. Anyone can have a win on the dogs, you know.'

'What about fingerprints?'

'Couper wore gloves.'

'Whaddya mean *Couper* wore gloves? What were you wearing?'

I don't answer.

'Christ, Mico. I honestly never thought I'd say this but I'm beginning to think that you're stupider than he is.'

'Look, it's okay. They've got no way of linking me to it unless Couper dobs me in—which he won't. Anyway, my fingerprints aren't on police file anywhere so if I stay clean from now on, they'll never track me down. I'm home free.'

Nina doesn't answer me straight away. I'm making a good argument. 'Well,' she finally says. 'I'll admit you're not totally fucked up right now, but you're not exactly what I'd call home free either.'

I don't get a chance to answer because a lady comes out.

'Miss Kartiniski.'

She looks friendly enough. Suppose it goes with the job. I stand up when Nina does but she puts her hand on my arm.

'On my own,' she says.

'But Neen—'

She doesn't acknowledge my protest. She just walks with obviously false confidence towards the white-coated woman who is about to examine her genitals. Shit, Nina actually looks nervous. That freaks me out a bit.

I watch her leave the room and then I sit back down. I know what she's thinking. I know what we've both been thinking. Neither of us have ever mentioned the 'C' word. She's kept working and I've kept drinking and we've both kept hoping. We've always carried on as if nothing was really wrong. But today, sitting here on my own in this place that's too clean with all these posters around with slogans like 'pap smear every two years', it doesn't feel like nothing's wrong. And I bet Nina's going to feel like something's bloody well wrong when she's lying back with her legs spread apart and some stranger poking around inside her, asking the most personal questions you can ask someone. Poor Neen.

I sit there for less than an hour and then Neen comes out. I can't tell whether the news is good or bad from the look on her face. She doesn't look me in the eye. It's as if I'm not there. It's as if nobody's there—or at least that she doesn't want to look in case anyone is. She makes another appointment with the woman at reception and we leave. She doesn't say a word until we get to the car. And then the only word she says is no.

'You want me to drive?' I say, and she says 'no'.

Three sets of lights later she starts talking.

'They're pretty sure I have something called endometriosis.'

I ask her what that means.

'It means I'm not dying or anything like that, but it explains why sometimes I feel like I am.'

'What do you mean: feel like you're dying?'

'Like nearly every time I've done a poo for the last two weeks I've ended up lying on the fuckin' floor okay?'

'Oh.'

I didn't realise that she was in that much pain. I mean, I knew she was in pain, but I didn't understand quite how much. I don't know what to say, and Neen obviously doesn't feel like talking anyway. Usually we fight to get a word in on each other but this afternoon we're resigned to listening to the engine of her car and the wind whipping in through my open window. Just like it was the night I quit my service station job, when I was in that trance. I wonder whether Neen's in some sort of trance as well. After all, she's had a pretty intense experience. Maybe she's a bit numb right now. Maybe too numb to even care about that cold wind coming in. I know how that can be. When you can't think beyond the shock you're in.

'Close the window, can you? And try and think about what you want for dinner. We should stop and pick up something while we're out.'

I wind the window up. 'Is there something you can do? I mean—to make things better?'

'Maybe. They want me to have something called a laparoscopy.'

'A what? What is it? Will it fix it?'

Neen sighs. 'It'll help them see what's going on inside me. And then maybe they can do something about it.

'What the fuck's going on inside you?'

'They reckon I'm bleeding.'

'What? Bleeding inside? Right now you are?'

'I don't know about right now.'

'What do you mean you—'

'Look, can we talk about something else?'

'Sure. But you'll be okay, right?'

'I think so.'

I can't think of anything else to talk about so I keep my mouth shut. There's a strange mood in the car. It's a sense of tension mixed up with a sense of relief. Almost as if we both know that she's not totally fucked up right now but it's not exactly what you'd call being home free either.

Chapter twenty-one
Road trip

The last thing I want to see as we pull up at home is the purple Kingswood.

Correction.

The last thing I want to see is my dad standing on the porch. He doesn't say anything as we get out of Nina's car and walk up our driveway but he's got the same look on his face as he did when we went around to Mr Jessop's that time. Nina's in no mood to be involved in a family discussion. She grabs the bag of takeaway Thai from me and she says hello to Dad and when she doesn't get an answer she walks straight past him and lets herself into the house.

'Get in the car. We're going for a drive.'

'Hi Dad. I don't think so. I'm really not in the mood.'

He hardly moves a muscle on his face. 'Get in the car.'

'Really, Dad, no. We just got some tea and Nina's not feeling that well and I should maybe—'

'NOW MICO!'

He grabs my arm just above the elbow with a grip that

I imagine Janey's not altogether unfamiliar with, and fair nearly carries me down the driveway to his purple Kingswood. I'm still walking, sort of, but I swear the gravel isn't crunching beneath my feet, it's kind of scattering. And it's shattering under Dad's heavy boots.

I twist my neck around to see Neen watching from the doorway. I manage to yell that I'm sorry and that I'll be back soon, before Dad manhandles me into the car. She gives a small half-sympathetic, half-dismissive wave that seems to simultaneously say she understands but she's got enough on her mind already to really give a shit. I don't get a chance to wave back to her because she's shut the front door by the time Dad's transferred his grip from me to the steering wheel and his stomp from the gravel to the Kingswood's accelerator. The tyres spin a little as we pull away. I feel it in my guts.

'So. Where to, Mico?' my dad asks, sarcastic spittle dripping from his lip. 'Should we go and see what's on at the drive-in?'

I feel a spin in my guts again, only this time it's not the tyres—it's actually my guts spinning.

'Um, no, not really. I should be getting back. Neen's not well and—'

'Did she enjoy the movie the other night, then?'

'Umm. Yeah, I think so,' I say, in a less convincing voice than if I had been trying to tell my father I was a Buddhist nun and that I moonlighted as a Formula One driver during the Christmas season.

My dad momentarily loses control of the steering wheel as he flings his left arm around to give me an almighty smack in the side of the head. We swerve onto the wrong side of the road, but I'm less worried about the oncoming traffic than I am about losing my hearing. My ear feels like it's had a goddamn electric current put through it. I rub the side of my head in silence as Dad pulls us back to where we should be.

'Jesus Christ, Mico.' His face is trembling he's so angry. 'What do you think I am—stupid?'

I have to sit there another few minutes to work up the courage to speak.

'Where are we going?' I eventually ask.

He doesn't answer, just keeps driving. Bastard. He never tells me where we're going at times like this. I wonder how he found out about the robbery. Maybe I did tell Bob the butcher after all. Bloody hell, my face is stinging from that backhander. I don't particularly feel like another one so I sit tight and wait for my Dad to say something. When I get bored doing that I stare out of the window and watch the sun go down behind the hills that line the side of the freeway.

An hour later we're still driving. Dad looks calmer. More focused. Hasn't said a word to me since he went quiet. We're heading back in the direction of his house. It's quite dark. Closer to home, Dad pulls into the local drive-thru bottle shop.

'What do you want?' he says.

'What?'

'What beer do you—'

'Melbourne Bitter,' I say. 'Longnecks.'

'A slab of Melbourne Bitter cans,' says my dad to the bloke bending at the car window. I don't know what's going on here and I doubt Dad's going to tell me. He pays the man and doesn't say anything. Then we stop at a service station to pick up, of all things, a bag of firewood. Then we drive home. As I'm carrying the carton in, I'm thinking about those Melbourne cans. I really feel like one now. Mum opens the door for us. She looks worried.

'Nina's been on the phone. Where have you been?'

'Driving,' says Dad.

'What's going on, Stan?'

'Nothing.'

'What happened to your face, Mico?'

I catch sight of it in the hallway mirror. There's a massive red mark creeping from my ear to my jaw. It looks like an Eric Papadopoulos special.

'Nothing. How's Nina?'

'She didn't sound too happy.'

I don't know why but I ask Mum to go over and hang out with Neen. I've never asked her to do anything like that before and I can tell by the look on her face that she's as surprised as I am. But she manages to regain her composure.

'Well,' she says. 'I suppose if you're going to be here with your Dad, I could. I suppose.' She wanders off down the hall to get changed. I tell Dad if I'm going to be much longer then I'm going to have to ring Nina.

'You've got five minutes,' he says. 'And bring that bag of wood out the back yard when you've finished.'

Neen picks up after half a ring.

'Mico. You all right? Where are you?'

I ask if she's okay and she says she's felt better but at the end of the day she's glad she knows what the problem is. I tell her that I don't really know what's happening, except that I'm at my parents' house and I'm about to have a beer with my dad.

'You're what?'

I tell her that my mum's on her way over for a chat.

'She's *what*?'

I tell her I don't understand any more than she does but that we're just going to have to go with the flow. I tell her I'll be home as soon as I can and that I'm thinking of her and that I'm sorry I'm not there. There must be something about the tone of my voice because she says it's okay and that I should go and talk with my dad and I can tell she means it.

I hang up the phone as Mum's car starts in the driveway. I grab the bag of wood and drag it out the back, where there's a tub full of ice and beer cans. There's also half a forty-gallon drum, a stack of newspapers and a pile of sticks. Dad's standing next to the drum with a beer in his hand and a faded, rusty silver medallion around his neck. Oh God, I think. Not again.

Chapter twenty-two
Talking heads

Dad doesn't muck around. He's straight into it. Building the fire, that is. Part of me is dying to make a smart comment about that goddamn medallion. But there's another part of me that wants to keep quiet and watch my daggy dad scrunch up last week's *Sunday Mail* and try to place it just right in the bottom of the drum. That doesn't want to tell the old man that for fuck's sake you can throw it in basically any bloody way and it will still fucking burn. There's a part of me that, for once, just wants to shut-up and watch.

And drink. The Melbourne's going down a treat. Sure gives you a bit of a chill though. I'm looking forward to that fire all right. I sit back on one of our old deckchairs and let my mind drift. I'm not that worried about where the conversation might eventually head. I don't know why. It just feels like things couldn't go anywhere that I wouldn't be able to handle right now.

Dad's putting in the kindling. Placing it just right, I guess. I don't know. I can't see. I can only assume. I look at the dark grass at my feet and wonder how Nina's doing. And suddenly the fire's roaring and I have to move my chair a few feet back next to Dad who's sat down and is sipping on his beer.

'And that's how you build your own fire son,' he says.

'She's a beauty,' I say. 'A real rip-roarer, Dad.' I'm being serious now.

'I don't want to talk any shit, Mico.'

And that's it. The only things moving in that back garden for the next half an hour are the beating flames and the slowly warming beer cans that seem to raise themselves to our lips every so often. The only sounds are a steady roar from the drum and the odd awkward swallow or creaking of tin. Then Dad breaks our silence.

'I think something's wrong with me toenail,' he says. He takes his boot and his sock off. 'Have a look at that. See?'

He might be right. His nail's looking pretty dodgy.

'How long's it been like that?'

'Since I stubbed it on Jessop's patio. I nearly ripped the whole bloody thing off. I think it might be getting infected or something.'

He takes off his other boot and sock and, infected toenail or not, he's starting to look pretty comfortable so I decide to take off my shoes and socks too. We sit there warming our feet by the drum. Every so often Dad gets up to stoke the fire and we sit there and talk about shit and drink beer.

When we knock off a few more cans, Dad says he's all beered out and that he's going to have a nip of port instead and do I want one too or am I going to stay on the beers? I tell him I'll have both thanks. We've set a fairly cracking pace and I'm a little bit pissed. As he's pouring a dash of port he asks me about what happened the other night with Bob the butcher. Somehow I knew he'd find out about that. Bob the butcher has a big mouth.

I tell Dad that I went to the front bar looking for him. That I went looking for *him*. I can tell though, that Dad's not asking that question. He's asking about what Bob the butcher must have told him.

I can't remember exactly what I told Bob the butcher and so I don't know exactly what to tell my dad and so I tell him exactly everything. The van crash, Janey and Couper, Aaron, the robbery, the ex-crim with the opener, the deaf guy—everything. The port is smooth and the beer is cold and my lips are loose and my dad is all ears. I talk for ages and he doesn't say much at all. When I look up I see my mum is back and she's pulled up a seat as well. I don't know how long she's been listening. I don't care anyway. We all sit and stare at the fire until Mum says something.

'Nina's exhausted, poor thing,' she says. 'She's gone to bed. Perhaps we should too, guys.'

'Good idea,' says Dad. 'Help me with these shoes will you dear?'

'Oh, how's your toe?' says Mum.

'Better than it's going to be, I think. You want to stay here tonight, Mico?'

'Nah, I'll walk home.' I ask if it's all right if I sit a while and finish off my drinks. Dad says I can sit there all night if I want to. Just keep an eye on the drum. I raise my beer can in a cheers to him and Mum and listen to them go in through the sliding back door.

The fire's dying. There's just one long piece of wood that's sticking out. I only shoved that in a while ago. I pull it out by the top which is still cold and I hold it up against the night sky. It's long and thin with a thick growth at one end. It almost looks like an oar. 'The Oar-lympic torch,' I chuckle to myself. I decide to take it with me when I walk home. To light the way. I sit there for another ten minutes or so and I finish off my beer and my port. Then I tip the rest of the ice from the tub into Dad's fire. I leave in a reasonably good mood with the drum hissing and smoking and I set off down the driveway with my torch.

It's going to be daylight very soon. I won't be needing the torch for long. Not that you could really say it's much use anyway. The big fat glowing ember on the end could hardly be said to be lighting up the night. It looks hot enough though. I hold the torch out and laugh and tell myself I'm going to build my own fire, whatever the fuck that means.

When I get to Jessop's house, instead of just passing, I stop and lean on the fence. That dirty old bastard, I think to myself. I really should have kicked him in the guts that day. Taught him a lesson like my dad did. I stand

180

there and I stare at his house and think maybe I should lob some rocks through the window or something and then I think fuck it, he's not worth it and then I hear a crackle.

The fat glowing ember on the end of my stick has fallen off and set Mr Jessop's long dry front lawn on fire. It's pretty overgrown now that Dad's stopped going around to mow it. Oh shit, I think, and bolt around to try and stamp the flames out. But I only manage to shake more red-hot embers off my stick. Now there are six or seven spot fires happening and the grass is whistling and singing like the birds overhead that are starting to signal the start of a brand new day. And I'm drunk off my face and I've got to make a decision so I pick up the biggest rock I can see and I lob it at Jessop's front window and I drop the torch and do a pretty quick dash/stumble out of there, hoping the sound of breaking glass will wake Jessop and that he'll call the bloody fire brigade or something.

I run all the way home and the whole time I'm freaking out about how I'm going to tell Neen and whether I should call the cops or the fire brigade and whether anyone saw me. I'm not much of a runner at the best of times and, after all that beer and port and God knows how many cigarettes, I'm feeling really crap when I get home. I head straight for the couch. I don't think I even bother shutting the door.

Dad's port must have a bit of a kick in it. I'm trying to work out a plan but it's too hard when the room's spinning like it is. I pick up the phone and try to call the fire brigade but I can't even hit the right buttons with my finger. I have to make the room stop spinning before I can do anything at all so I lay my head back on the couch and shut my eyes. I don't know how long it is before I drop into a deep drunken slumber, far away from the world that continues on around me.

Sometimes I have particularly strange dreams when I'm drunk. This morning is one of those times. I have the strangest dream when I'm lying asleep on that couch. I dream that Ben McPhenton is in my living room in his police uniform. 'Millevic,' he's saying. 'Millevic, wake up.' He's saying it in a dream voice and wearing some kind of dream face. In my dream I wake up and he tells me my friend's been involved in an accident. I tell him don't be stupid, Jessop's not my friend. But he's right about it being an accident, I tell him. Then McPhenton says it was serious. That my friend might not walk again. I tell him I already know that and I agree that Eric Papadopoulos is my friend. I tell him he should see the guy bounce down stairs. He tells me I can keep dreaming if I want but that I should go to the hospital when I wake up and visit my friend. I smile and I tell him that I've already been to the hospital to visit Nina. Just the other day. And I tell him she's my lover as well as my friend so technically he's wrong on that count as well. Then Ben McPhenton stands there for a few moments, puts his hat on and says he'll be on his way then and that he hopes I take care of myself. That's when I start laughing out loud and I really know I'm dreaming because he sounds like he gives a fuck for once.

Chapter twenty-three
I don't know what I been told

The first thing I think about when I wake up is food. I feel crook in the guts and that's a pretty rare thing for me. Man, I must have put away a few beers. Five minutes later I'm standing naked in the kitchen, gingerly scraping burnt bits off my toast. I can't think straight. My brain feels waterlogged. It's like a full car park. It won't let me take in any new information until an old bit of information finds a way out. All I can think about is putting the butter and the peanut paste on my toast and forcing the tepid scraped multigrain hunks into my mouth, which is drier than a desert skeleton.

I munch. Ever so slowly. Start to fill my burning vacant stomach with something mildly solid. It takes a few minutes for my brain to accept that my stomach is being attended to. Then something screeches into my head and blares its horn so loud my eyeballs throb: I started a fire.

I say 'fuck' out loud to myself. And now I don't just feel crook in the guts. I feel crook all over.

'Oh. Very sexy. Show us your man-boobs why don't ya?'

'Hey, Neen.'

She comes over and starts dusting crumbs off my chest. She smiles. 'Look at you. All nice and cuddly.'

I push her hand away. Not angrily, just firmly enough for her to know I'm not currently in the frame of mind where I feel like having a laugh about the fact that I'm getting a little podgy around the upper chest. Nina's in some sort of good mood though. She drops her hands and starts to gently tickle my cock.

'Oh baby, don't worry. I like your little boobs. I wouldn't have you any other way.'

'Neen, leave it out.'

'You're the one leaving it out, honey.'

Her tickling fingers join together to form a firm grip. She turns away and looks back over her shoulder and gives me a gentle tug. I wish I felt good enough to let her lead me into the bedroom. Good enough to lie down with her. But I don't feel at all good. I feel terrible. My brain feels like it's been ripped out and thrown against a brick wall. I need to stay still, to focus.

'What's wrong, honey?'

I don't say anything straight away. I'm trying to sort out the thought jam in my head.

'Mico?'

'Neen. Listen to me. I think I got too drunk last night. I think I might have started a fire.'

'What do you mean?'

'At Jessop's house.'

'What the hell were you doing at Jessop's house?'

'I don't know.'

'Oh shit, Mico.'

'Neen, I didn't mean to. I swear I didn't. I was just pissed is all.'

I'm looking at her clearly now. One of the things about how Neen doesn't miss anything is that she has a way of knowing when I'm being straight with her as well as when I'm up to something. And so she immediately knows I'm telling the truth.

'Okay.' She's calm. How the fuck does she do it? 'Let's go visit your parents. We'll drive past Jessop's on the way and check it out. Do you remember exactly what happened?'

'Not really.'

'Did anyone see you?'

I shrug. No one would have been up at that time. It must have been about five o'clock or something. Even Mrs Beveringham doesn't usually clock on until about seven.

'Well, get some clothes on, baby. We'll go and check it out.'

I go into the bedroom and struggle into a pair of jeans. All these bad thoughts keep running through my head. The sort of running that soldiers do at boot camp. Slogging through mud and marsh for hours on end with backpacks weighing a ton. That's how these thoughts are running through my head. Stomping through my already aching brain:

I don't know what I been told (I don't know what I been told)

Mico burnt down somebody's goddamn house last night when he was drunk.

I don't know what sort of damage I might have done. Maybe I've completely gutted the place. And then there's bloody Jessop. Christ, if he was there I might have even killed him. Maybe the cops are around at my parents' house right now, looking for me.

Shit.

My parents.

Whether that fire was big or not, they would have guessed that I had something to do with it. That's one thing I can be sure about. Christ. When Dad was talking about building my own fire, I'm pretty goddamn sure he didn't mean for me to burn down some guy's house, even if the guy *had* been having a perve at his daughter.

I don't want to go to my parents' house. Not now. Maybe not ever again. I pull my t-shirt over my head to see Neen standing in the doorway.

'And don't start having second thoughts about going to visit your parents either,' she says. 'You are going to deal with this and you are going to deal with them.'

'I need a beer.'

'The fuck you do. Honey, I hardly ever tell you not to drink but I'm telling you today. You need your head clear. Do you understand me? This is serious.'

I follow her out to her car. I'm feeling sicker by the minute. Neen speaks more gently as she opens the car door. 'Don't get too worried. We don't even know what we're in for yet.'

When we round the corner that leads into Mum and Dad's street I start thinking I'm really going to heave my guts up. But it's not because the situation is getting worse, it's because I suddenly feel sick with relief. I can see that Jessop is as alive and well as he's ever been. He's in his Thai dragon dressing gown. Standing on the side of the road, talking to Mrs Beveringham. Looking at what used to be his house. Thank Christ, I think. At least I'm not a murderer.

Not entirely true. I killed a house. It's a charred mess. There's still smoke or steam or something rising from the ashes. I can't look for long because as soon as they hear Nina's car, Beveringham and Jessop turn and stare at us. I don't know if they're stares of suspicion or knowledge or neither but they're enough to jolt my own gaze from the blackened wreck that is Mr Jessop's house down to the wide grey bumpy strip that is the road in front of us.

My parents must have heard our car pull up. Mum opens the front door.

I start blurting out an apology before she has a chance to say anything, but then I stop because I see Janey in the hallway behind Mum. She's been crying. Maybe she still is. I can't really tell.

'Janey. What the hell are you doing here?'

'Come inside guys,' says Mum.

Nina and me follow Mum and Janey down the hall to the dining room where Dad is.

'Dad,' I say. 'I'm really sorry.'

'It's okay, Mico.' He looks grave. 'We'll talk later.'

Is this it? Is this the extent of crap that I'm going to cop from my parents for burning down a fucking house? I'd almost laugh if it wasn't for the looks on their faces. Mum tells us to sit down. Janey starts to cry quietly. It's the power I can sense behind her restrained sob that wakes my brain up.

'What's going on?'

And they tell me. I'm not sure how I react. I'm not sure I even feel Nina's hand resting on my shoulder. All I am sure of is that I somehow want to switch them off like a TV. Turn their volume down. Change the channel. Do something, because I hate what I'm hearing.

Chapter twenty-four
Sleeping Ugly

It's three days before I can bring myself to go and see him.

It's a Sunday afternoon. Normally we'd be kicking back in our favourite beer garden right about now. But instead we're here. It's hard to know what to feel when I look at him. He was all alone with the respiratory machine when Janey and Neen first brought me in. The poor bastard. His eyes aren't wicked. They're shut. He's not talking shit or telling stories. For Christ's sake, he's not even breathing by himself.

At first I stand back as if I'm looking at a piece of art or something. I walk around him, keeping my distance, as if there's an invisible barrier between us. I almost chide Janey for walking straight over and touching his hand, but then I follow her lead and get closer. I try and convince myself that the man beneath the mask is my mate Couper. And I try to convince myself that it's not.

I wonder how many times he would have looked at someone the way he's being looked at now. How many times he's seen another human being lying there like a lump. Lifeless. I know it's not quite the same. I mean, he's not dead. It's just that right now, he may as well be—and he definitely would be if it wasn't for all the fancy bloody machines everywhere.

'Hang in there Couper. You'll be okay.'

I'm disgusted with how weak my voice sounds. I sound like I don't mean it. And in a way, I don't. It's not that I think he won't be okay, it's just that it seems pointless saying such a thing to someone in a coma. I keep the soppy encouragement to a bare minimum after that. In fact, I don't say anything else at all on that first visit. Not to Couper, or anyone. I just turn and walk out.

I smoke cigarettes by the car until Neen joins me and we leave. We don't say much. We stop at the beer garden on our way home and have a couple of quiet beers. And we buy one for Couper and put it on the table and leave without drinking it. On the way out we run into one of those detectives who'd been asking questions. He recognises us and he tells us how it all went down. How Couper got screwed in the end.

Now we know why the cops didn't find any money at his house or at the hotel. It was never there. Couper had it hidden in his 'new' car which he hadn't even told me and Neen about. The cops traced the car back to its old owner and found out that Couper bought it the day after the robbery. Paid a thousand bucks cash for the heap of shit. It was probably the first thing he bought. I should have known Couper couldn't live without wheels for long.

I guess I should have also known he was always going to get caught. The cops started tailing Couper shortly after he was first questioned. And if you're tailing someone as reckless as Couper you're never going to have to wait too long for them to fuck up. And sure enough, early one morning Couper rolled out of some dodgy all-night pub to get some more money from the back seat of his car, money that he was keeping in a stolen calico bag with 'Burroughs and Sons' stamped on it. The stupid idiot held it out in full view of the whole fucking street while he rifled through for a fifty. In full view of the two surveillance guys who were dogging him. Then he chucked the bag back through the rear window and went back into the pub. Turns out he wasn't going for more beer. He was just nicking back in quickly to pay off a bet, and then he was straight back out. Anyway, the surveillance guys called the detectives who got there in a matter of minutes. Coups didn't even see them approaching as he hopped behind the wheel of his very own Datsun 180B rustbucket. Had he seen them he probably would have led them on a mock chase, hitting the highway at 30 k's and laughing his head off as they pulled him over and took him away. But the detectives didn't get a chance to pull him over, because when Couper pulled out of his parking space, he was drunk enough to forget to check if anything was coming. And the guy driving the furniture truck was too busy trying to light his cigarette to really be watching the road and the Datsun 180B pulling out in front of him. So he didn't even know Couper was there until he heard the Datsun split apart.

The cops never recovered all the money. When Couper's car split, the calico bag got thrown into the street and the notes blew away. Those standers-by with strong enough consciences helped collect any money they could and returned it to the police. In the end, the cops retrieved about two grand. Less than Couper had on him the first time they questioned him. Perhaps it was enough though, to stop them looking for anyone else. As things stand now, the only question the detective's asking is if me and Neen are coping okay. I tell him we're doing the best we can, and I guess I'm telling him the truth. But it's easier for us. We've got each other. I'd hate to go through this alone.

Janey doesn't want to go through it alone either. She's decided to move back in with Mum and Dad for the time being. She's also going back to school next week. Mum and Dad have promised to back off a bit. They still reckon the best thing for Janey at the moment is to get on with her life, but even they understand that for her, getting on with life is going to mean visiting Couper on weekends instead of doing extra homework. As for babysitting, nobody's mentioned it, but if Janey ends up staying with Couper in the long term, she's going to have to do a fair bit of it. The doctors don't reckon Couper's going to be able to do much for himself for a long time, if ever. Somehow though, even when they put it like that, the reality of the whole situation still doesn't hit home.

When it does hit home is the next time I'm visiting Couper and I bump into his parents. I haven't seen them in years, and yet I can still tell they've aged tremendously since the accident. The poor bastards already have one son in jail, and now it looks as if their other son is going to be trapped in his own body for the rest of his life. Mr Couper's hair looks as if it has literally turned grey overnight. It's like a big housepaint-thick grey wig. I can tell he hasn't shut his eyes properly for days. Mrs Couper looks like she's been hit by a truck herself. She's like a marionette or something. All the life has gone out of her limbs, all the blood drained from her face. It's all she can do to shuffle over and whisper hello before she flops into a chair as if someone was dragging her with invisible strings. We've never really spoken to each other properly and in that hospital room we're not about to start. It's strange seeing the two of them. Strange standing in that room with them and avoiding talking about their son while listening to the machine help him breathe. I know I should try and say something positive but it seems like it would be even more pointless than the piss-weak encouragement I tried to give to Couper. At least he has no idea of what he looks like.

I leave Couper's parents to be alone with him and the machines.

I catch a bus home and for the first time in a long time I don't notice the other passengers or the noise at all. When I get home I sit on the couch with a beer. Bob Sanders and the sausage chick are on the telly with the dogs again. I wonder if Bob Sanders would remember Couper. I wonder if he remembers the night we crashed the van. Probably not. He was more pissed than the rest of us. It's amazing we survived. As accidents go, it was a pretty bad one. And I should know, I've been in a few.

That night with Aaron was an accident of sorts. In a way, he was my guy driving the furniture truck. I didn't even see him coming. I mean, sure, I can look back now and say it was all part of growing up, but I couldn't then. I was just a kid. I didn't know what life could throw at you. I didn't know I had to make those choices. I wasn't ready to make them. And though I've been angry at Aaron for the last few years, I've been angry at myself too. I know I should never have got so blind drunk in the first place. I shouldn't have let myself be in that position, where I couldn't see something like that coming.

I look at Bob Sanders yapping away on the screen in front of me. Yapping away like the Scottish terrier that belongs to some old lady he's trying to interview. The camera pans down and the Scottish terrier's got so excited he's doing a piss. Bob Sanders fake laughs and says he doesn't know if the Scottish terrier's quite ready to join the gruelling dog show circuit yet. He's about to say something else but I change channels because I'm sick of Bob Sanders and pissing Scottish terriers. Then I turn off the TV because I'm sick of it altogether. Sick of sitting on this couch. Sick of doing nothing.

Chapter twenty-five
Obwigation fwee

Mum and Dad said that Constable Ben McPhenton con-
tacted them. Apparently he said he was concerned about
me and that he came around to my house after Couper's
accident. He wasn't on official business or anything, he
was just doing me a favour. Thought I might want to know
that my best mate was fighting for his life in hospital.
Apparently I wasn't making much sense. Apparently I
mumbled something about a Jessica or an Eric or someone called Dean. I can't remember exactly what I said to
him that morning. I was still smashed and seven-eighths
asleep. I know what I'll say next time I see him though.
I'll say sorry for always assuming he didn't give a fuck.

Couper still hasn't woken up. They've moved him to
a rehab centre. I don't know how many weeks it's been.
I keep feeling like I'm going to run out of things to say to
him, but I haven't yet. Today I've been going through
some of the funny things that have happened to us over the
years. When I started off I thought maybe I'd be able to
make him laugh. I thought maybe I could even get him to

open his mouth and make a smart comment so I could tell him to shucking fut up. Right now I'd settle for him opening his eyes and stopping his dribbling.

Couper's friend Caroline is one of the carers here. She's a top girl. She's always dancing around Couper's room, singing to him, whenever she's doing anything in there. Couper's right. She's a bloody good dancer. Not a bad voice either. She's got another one of those talent competitions coming up soon. I told her I'd be along to watch. She said no worries as long there were no more fights.

Dad was just here. Him and Mum have been visiting Couper regularly. I don't know why, I never thought they liked him that much. Dad reckons he's just helping Couper and his family run a few miles. Dad won't be running anywhere himself for a while though. His toe's infected. He's had to cut a hole in his sneaker just to give it a bit of air. He asked how Neen was getting on so I told him she's had a few holes cut in her as well. She had her laparoscopy last week. She's got these four little scars on her now, like points of an invisible cross. A sort of reminder of what she's been bearing all this time. She's a lot happier already. It's funny, I always thought that I'd seen Neen as relaxed and happy as she could be but I didn't even know the half of it. Now that she's not walking around in constant pain she's like a different person. I suppose it's helping that she's been able to give up working for Mick the prick as well. She's been sleeping in for as long as me, lately. Or maybe I've been getting up earlier.

We've got plenty of money left but it won't be too long before at least one of us will have to go back to work. I think it's my turn. I've got a Centrelink appointment this afternoon. 'Intensive job-seeking assistance' or something like that. I'm happy to go. Anyway, it'll give me something new to talk to Couper about.

I hang around with Couper a couple of days a week. He's in his own room in a private hospital now. He's even got his own balcony, not that he knows it. I can go out there and smoke and lean in through the door to keep talking to him. I spend most of my time out there smoking and leaning in through the door. It's a weird conversation, the one between the conscious and the unconscious. There's only so long you can sustain it before things break down. Only so many unanswerable questions you can ask: Remember that mate? Yeah? I bet you fucking do. What do you reckon we go and do that again when you get better? Yeah? You'd like that? Yeah?

Yeah, yeah. Right now I bet he doesn't remember or reckon anything. His parents have stuck up some old photos of him from when he was a kid. I didn't know him then. He looked like a cheeky bastard though. 'Jeez mate, I never realised what a cheeky little bastard you looked like when you were young. Ugly little fucker too, eh?'

I'm nearly out of one-way conversation for today. Nearly out of being able to tolerate silence. Nearly out of smokes. I've got my Centrelink appointment in less than an hour so I do the bolt. 'See ya soon Coups.'

I head off down the corridor. It's overflowing with fluorescent white light and strangely empty of other people. There are no bustling doctors and nurses at this place. There are no emergencies. No life or death situations. At a rehab centre every room's got someone like Couper in it. The corridor walls are covered with paintings done by patients—people who have to hold the paintbrush in their mouth because they've lost all use of their limbs, or who can paint using their left hand but can only muster the energy for thirty minutes a day. The paintings make the place look like open day at kindergarten. It's the artistic equivalent of a talent contest. I wonder if I'll ever get to hear Couper hanging shit on the artists. Or whether he'll just become one of them.

I get to the Centrelink office with a few minutes to spare and sit there and wait for my name to be called. When I hear it I look up, and lo and behold, it's my old mate Neville and he's still just got the one earring. It turns out he really is a decent bloke and I leave with a phone number and the name of a service station that's hiring at the moment. But as much as I'm ready to go back to work, there's something about going back to the world of service stations that's not sitting quite right. I tell this to Neen when I get home.

She says it sounds like I'm making up more excuses not to get on with life. I try to convince her I'm not and so she tells me to prove it. She makes me promise to take the next job that comes my way. And not just that, I have to ask everyone I come into contact with if they've got anything going.

'I promise,' I say. 'Just no fucking service station work.'

'And you have to go and explain to earring-boy that you're really looking to get out of that line of work and ask him whether he can help you get on some sort of career path.'

'Sure. Anything else?'

'Well, I don't know,' she laughs. 'How about a massage?'

'No worries,' I say. 'I'll just get myself a beer.'

So Neen makes herself comfortable on the floor and I set myself up with a beer and then I sit over her lower back and start rubbing her shoulders. I'm looking up at our magnificent dried flower garden when the phone rings. I can reach it from where I am.

'Hello?'

'Hewwo. I'm just cawing to tell you about our obwigation fwee twip to New Zeawand.'

'Oh, for Christ's sake.'

Neen twists her head around and asks who it is. I put my hand over the mouthpiece and tell her it's the same bloody home loans guy who's rung twice already. 'The Mr Magoo guy.' I tell her I'm going to blow him off for good this time.

'No you're not,' she says. 'Remember your promise.'

Goddamn Neen. She's a fucking stickler.

Actually she's more than that. She's the driver of the goddamn bus. And I suddenly realise I've been riding it for the last two years. Hell, I got off the side of the road on the night that we met. She let me bring my beer and she's been steering me in the right direction ever since. I rub her shoulder with one hand and make a grab for the wheel with the other. It's my turn to drive for a while.

Three days later I find myself in an office drinking tepid coffee from a foam cup. I'm known as 'new guy'. I've done a frantic two-day training course and they think I'm ready to start actually working the phones. I'm not worried. If I can rob a bloody funeral parlour with only half an hour's planning, I figure I can get people to a home-loan seminar with a couple of days training.

'You're on that phone over there,' says some guy, I think his name is Dave. He's got a really bad *Home and Away* hairstyle and a mischievous smile.

'Sure.'

The phone looks bloody archaic.

'You know what to do?'

'Sure.'

'I'll watch your first call, okay?'

I put the receiver to my ear and push the automatic dialling button. I look back over my shoulder. 'Why don't I get to use a headset, like in training?'

'We haven't got enough yet. New guys have to use the phones for now.'

'Sure.' It rings three or four times and someone answers.

'Hello?'

'Hi there. I'm just calling to sa—Ow! Fuck! Jesus!'

'I beg your pardon?'

I hang up. My tongue is burning. I got some sort of electric shock from the receiver. I look around to see Dave having a right old laugh. When he's finished he tells me there's something wrong with this particular phone. Apparently the cheap bastard who runs the place does his own servicing. 'When your tongue gets too near the receiver you risk getting a slight electric shock. Not enough to kill you or anything,' he says. 'But enough to wake you up, new guy.'

Fuck this, I think. First thing tomorrow I'm looking for something else. But today I have to keep my promise. 'Is there anything I can do to avoid it?'

'Just hold your tongue down flat against the bottom of your mouth,' he says, 'so it doesn't get near the receiver. And don't worry—as soon as the next new guy comes in we'll move you to another phone, maybe even a headset, depending on how you go.'

'Sure.' I hit the autodial again. Press my tongue down flat. Sigh.

'Hello?'

'Hewwo. I'm cawing to see if you'd wike the chance to win an obwigation fwee twip to New Zeawand.'

'Obligation what?'

'Obwigation fwee.'

Acknowledgements

The 'this-couldn't-have-happened-without-you' thanks go to Mara Laszczuk and Margarita Biezaite. I love you both dearly.

Special thanks to the rest of my fantastic family and my unbelievably good friends, who've always given me lifts when the bus service was down, to Peta Kruger for three precious years and to Wilbert Warren Woodlich, a little-known white trash caravan park manager who helped me kick Death out of a pub once.

And to Malcolm St James, thanks for the perspective, Detective.

Many thanks also to: Professor Tom Shapcott for his unfailing support and excellent creative advice; Gina Inverarity, who helped with the editing stuff what we done on the book (the one what you all just read); Vicky Machen, Dr Ramona Chryssidis and Rob Gregory for their time and expertise; my 2003 classmates Leanne Amodeo, Rebekah Clarkson, Judy Clothier, Sam Franzway, Rosemary Jackson, Sharon Kernot, Elizabeth Lau and Gay Lynch who all contributed to the forming of this book; Kerri Franz and Sandra Spry for doing such a good job with me; the tuff putts crew—I salute you all; Wakefield Press for putting the book out; and, of course, thanks to the Festival Awards judges. You can pick your families up in three weeks.

In memory of

Shannon Klauber
Craig Elphick
Cheyne Gelagin
Tim Morton
Alan Wheaton

(beautiful men/silly bastards)

Street Furniture

Matt Howard

Street Furniture is a hilarious, feel-good book about a guy who's languished forever (more or less happily) unemployed with his mates in the suburbs of Sydney. At 29 he somehow scores a publicist's job in a slick publishing firm in the city. He moves house, and hopes he won't lose his friends. And does true love await him?

'Matt Howard's spliff-happy, artful slacker of a hero Declan does to over-achieving what the Titanic did for boating. A funny, subtle and astute novel.' Shelley Gare

**** Australian Bookseller and Publisher

'Very much enjoyed it.' Magnus Fuxner

'Just gotta say: very impressed. Awesome!' Simon Proud

ISBN 1 86254 646 0

For more information visit www.wakefieldpress.com.au

Hill of Grace

Stephen Orr

1951. Among the coppiced carob trees and arum lilies of the Barossa Valley, old-school Lutheran William Miller lives a quiet life with his wife, Bluma, and son, Nathan, making wine and baking bread. But William has a secret. He's been studying the Bible and he's found what a thousand others couldn't: the date of the Apocalypse.

William sets out to convince his neighbours that they need to join him in preparation for the End. Arthur Blessitt, a Valley pioneer in floriculture, helps William deliver pamphlets and organise rallies. Others join the group but as the day approaches their faith is tested. The locals of Tanunda become divided. Did William really hear God's voice on the Hill of Grace? Did God tell him to preach the End of Days? Or is William really deluded?

The greatest test of all for William is whether Bluma and Nathan will support him. As the seasons pass in the Valley, as the vines flower and fruit and lose their leaves, William himself is forced to question his own beliefs and the price he's willing to pay for them.

ISBN 1 86254 648 7

For more information visit www.wakefieldpress.com.au

Wakefield Press is an independent publishing and
distribution company based in Adelaide, South Australia.
We love good stories and publish beautiful books.
To see our full range of titles, please visit our website at
www.wakefieldpress.com.au.

Fox Creek Wines   Government
of South Australia   A R T S A

Wakefield Press thanks Fox Creek Wines
and Arts South Australia for their support.